CHRISTMAS ON PALM COURT

AN ISLE OF PALMS SUSPENSE

STEPHANIE EDWARDS

To my parents and grandparents for
encouraging my love of reading and writing.

PART I

1

JULIA CAROLINE

1960

Candles flickered orange orbs onto the windows that lined Palm Court, and greenery accented with red ribbons decorated the alabaster doors. Julia Caroline pulled her blue cashmere shawl around her shoulders a little more tightly and adjusted her purse strap, wishing she had piled on more layers before leaving her home just moments earlier. The cap-sleeved poplin dress offered little warmth, but she didn't have time to think about the weather. She'd escaped without being noticed, a next to impossible feat with her parents and five siblings observing almost every move she made.

Drawing a deep breath, she closed her eyes for just a moment, allowing the peacefulness to seep into her soul. The swishing of tires sludging through the wet sand and shell drive brought her back to reality–a black Corvette idling at the edge of her driveway. As she tried to make out the driver's identity, the passenger door popped open, revealing her beau, James, who had leaned over to open the door for her.

He pushed his dark, wavy hair out of his eyes and flashed a

dimpled smile, sending her pulse racing. "Hop in, beautiful. Let's take my hot wheels for a spin."

Climbing into the impressive car, Julia Caroline admired the sleek black dash. "When did you get this?"

"Craziest thing ever ... my pops gave me the keys about an hour ago. He said it's an early Christmas and graduation gift. Whadya think?" He kissed her hand and stared into her eyes.

Shifting in her seat, she inched closer to the warmth of his body, resting her head on his shoulder. "It's super nice, but let's get outta here before anyone sees us. If my brother comes out the front door, he'll talk our ears off about his new chemistry set or something else equally boring."

He ran his hand down to the small of her back, taking her breath away. "Where do ya wanna go?"

She'd heard the question, but the sensation of his touch tingled down her spine. Regaining her composure, she bit her lip. "Anywhere away from here, and I don't want to come back ever again." Julia Caroline waved her hands in the air. What a divine concept! For the first time, she would be free. No more high school classes, babysitting her younger siblings or being the perfect daughter. At 18, she'd be her own person, finally. Of course, she'd be James' wife and, eventually, the mother to their children, but she had so many more goals than becoming a homemaker.

"You got it, baby. Let's burn some rubber." He put the car into first gear and peeled out.

She laughed. "You're being so casual about leaving and never coming back home. What gives?"

"Um, I thought you were joking. It would be wicked cool but not practical." He flicked the butt of a lit cigarette out the window and grinned at her. "We've got five more months of our senior year, and what about college? My pops is expecting me to take over the family medical practice. He'll be pretty ticked off if things don't go according to his plan. Medical school is going to take a while. Anyhow, the island needs a doctor, and it means we'll have a solid future. All of that's important, right?"

Julia wrinkled her nose. "Okay, maybe we can't just run away for good, but we could get married before anyone catches on. They don't even have to know that we are until we're ready to tell them. We could elope today in Charlotte, drive back like nothing happened, graduate in May and start college this fall." She jumped in her seat and clapped. "Hey, why don't we both go to school here instead? We could live in married student housing, too."

"Baby, you know I'll do anything for you, but–"

Pressing her body against his, she gazed upward into his eyes and batted her eyelashes. "If we got married today, we could finally ..."

Red-faced, James swerved onto the shoulder, slammed on the brake and stared at her with a grin. "Geez, Julia, what would your mother say if she heard you say that? Never mind, I've known her my whole life. I can tell you exactly what she'd say." In his best falsetto, he mocked Julia's mother. "'Julia Caroline, why, I never! That's the most unladylike thing I've heard all my life. Your grandmother would roll over in her grave if she heard the likes of this.' And she might not be wrong."

She pulled her body upright, placing her hands on her lap and clearing her throat. "Ahem, Mama says a lady shouldn't interfere in another woman's bedroom business, but she also says a true lady also waits until she is married to go to bed with her husband." Her plump lips flared. "If you're so bent on not getting hitched today, we'll wait. I just thought it would be nice to show you how much I love you. You're everything to me."

James sighed. "You know I love you, too. I just don't want us to mess up now; we're so close to finishing high school. Can we wait until June to get married? We can still sneak around and elope, or we could do the traditional thing and have a wedding with all the lace and flowers our mothers want."

"But I want to get married now. I don't care what our mamas want."

"That's not true, and what's the rush, anyway?" James wrapped his arm around her. "We've got all the time in the world."

A horn honking caught Julia Caroline's attention as a pale yellow car pulled up beside them. She drew a deep breath. "Speaking of the devil, or at least one of them, don't look now, but your mama's right beside us."

"What?" James turned his head, and Ethel Mason waved frantically, motioning for him to roll down his window. He grunted but complied. "Hello, Mama."

"I thought that was you, hon. Whatever are y'all doin' parked on the side of the road? What's the matter? I know that your brand new car hasn't broken down already." She straightened her already symmetrical strand of pearls and brushed off her shoulders with an impeccably white glove-covered hand.

"Nothin', Mama. We were just talking about colleges." James smiled.

"Well, for Heaven's sake, don't you think there are better places to discuss such matters than the side of the road in your brand new car that your daddy just gave you? He'd be so disappointed in that decision, young man. And Julia Caroline's mama wouldn't want her out here living on danger's doorstep either."

"Yes, ma'am. We're going to grab a bite to eat, and then we'll head straight home. See you there, Mama." He waved and bumped elbows with Julia Caroline, muttering "wave" under his breath. She moved her bare hand in a dainty motion, but then rubbed her elbow. *That hurt!*

"Thank you, son, for putting your poor mama's heart at ease. See you at home. Bye, kids. Ta, ta." She waved and drove away.

Julia Caroline sighed. "I guess that I can stop daydreaming

for right now. I'm just so ready to start our lives together. I want to get married the second we graduate. Deal?"

"I can't wait. It's going to be a blast, especially in the bedroom. Just because we can't do it yet doesn't mean it's not on my mind." James looked her up and down and winked. "Don't tell me you haven't thought about it."

Blushing, she giggled. "Oh, you! It wouldn't be ladylike for me to discuss such things, remember? Anyway, a lady never tells." She tickled his neck.

He pulled away. "Hey, I'm trying to get us back on the road, here! Give me a break!" James drummed his free hand on the steering wheel. "What do you want for dinner? Burgers or shrimp?"

"I want a milkshake more than just about anything in the world right now." She licked her lips and held her rumbling stomach in place.

"More than getting married?" he teased. "Just a few minutes ago, you were begging me to get hitched today. Did you change your mind?"

She tapped her chin with her index finger. "Hmm, which would I rather have–a frosty treat or a romantic evening with my husband? That's a difficult choice! I guess I'll go for the chocolate shake right now."

James lowered his sunglasses and peered over the top of the frames. "Not cool, not cool at all. Well, I guess I deserve that, seeing as how I asked you to wait for our wedding earlier. When we're married, I promise that I won't ask you to be patient ever again. Trust me, I want you, *all of you,* right now. I just want to make sure we're considering the big picture."

Playfully punching him on the arm, Julia Caroline laughed. "C'mon, just take me to get a burger, fries and a shake. We can figure out our future together later."

2

ELAINA
2021

"Hey, the Christmas parade floats are blocking the garage. Traffic is always a pain in Wilmington on parade days. I couldn't find a metered parking space until a minute ago, so I've been circling the block for half an hour. Why didn't you answer my texts? We're going to be late."

Elaina Nelson shook herself out of a trance, looking up at her fiancé. "Sorry. I fell asleep and had a weird dream. I didn't hear my phone."

Todd sighed, knelt in front of her and grabbed one of her feet, slipping on a red Kate Spade ballet flat and placing its mate on her other foot. Elaina laughed and steadied herself, holding onto his shoulder. "What are you doing?"

"Helping you finish getting ready. We should have left 15 minutes ago. You can do your hair and makeup in the car; c'mon, my parents are going to be pissed off if we're late." He opened the door to their condo and locked it behind them.

Walking outside, she patted her purse, a sleek black and white bag she'd inherited from her grandmother. A wave of nausea hit her, and she grabbed hold of the white railing on the front stoop. "Actually, I'm sorry. I don't think that I'm going to make it. I already feel carsick."

As they stepped back into the condo, Todd furrowed his brow. "What? We haven't even set foot in the car yet. How does that happen? Are you okay?" He placed his hand on her forehead. "You don't feel warm to me. Did you eat something weird for lunch?"

"Nope. I had puffed rice cereal with dried cranberries, not exactly an adventurous meal. Why don't you head on to the airport to pick up your mom and dad? I'll drink some ginger ale and take some medicine, and hopefully, I'll be back to normal by the time you guys get back here."

He took her hand. "But they're looking forward to seeing you, too. Are you sure you can't make the short ride?"

Her stomach gurgled, and she sighed. "I'd better not, but I'll put a pot of coffee on so it will be ready for your parents. They've had a long flight."

"Okay. Thanks, sweetie. Do you want me to stop and pick something up for you? Is there anything that would help?"

She kissed his cheek. "No–I've got everything I need here. Thanks."

"You can't help getting sick, but we can't miss the party tonight. Our whole family is in the same city at one time. That never happens."

"I know. Now, scoot, or you'll really be late." Elaina shooed him out the door. Wiping a thick bead of sweat from her brow, she popped a couple of antacids, chewing them and letting them settle before grabbing a ginger ale from the refrigerator. She sighed, collapsing into her overstuffed chair.

Maybe it was selfish, but Elaina had been dreading going to the airport all week. Had she made herself sick over it? Why had Todd made such a big deal about her going along to pick up his parents? It wasn't her first time to meet them, not even close. She'd known Jacqueline and Thomas Watts since her freshman year of college, when she had mistakenly been assigned as Todd's roommate in the boys' dormitory at their liberal arts college in small-town coastal North Carolina.

To their parents' chagrin, the school administration couldn't work out alternate sleeping arrangements for the first few school days. Jacqueline had insisted on sleeping on a cot in between them at night and raising hell with the dean during the day until student housing moved Elaina to her rightful room at the girls' dorm.

Luckily, Jacqueline's chaperoning didn't prevent Todd and Elaina from building a friendship. For the remainder of their first year, they studied together in local coffee shops and spent Saturdays kayaking through the tidal creeks or surfing at the beach. When the end of the school year rolled around, Todd took her to a secluded cove, where the mangroves painted a romantic backdrop. As they paddled into the hot-pink-hued sunset, he'd drawn a deep breath and professed his love for Elaina. Despite her concern for ruining their friendship, she'd admitted to reciprocating his feelings.

The sensation of snoring startled Elaina, jolting her awake. *Holy crap! When did I fall asleep? Shoot! I never finished getting ready.* She pulled herself out of the chair and slinked to the bathroom, applying a rose gold gloss to her thin lips and bronzer to her high cheekbones. Charcoal mascara accented her hazel eyes, and she pulled back her deep auburn curls with a nautilus shell clip. The pearl earrings and bracelet Todd had given her when they'd graduated were the finishing touches.

Right after she sat down again, the front door popped open, "Hey, honey, we're back." Todd and his parents filed inside.

Jacqueline pushed her way to Elaina, her arms spread wide. "Sugar, it's simply been ages since I've seen your divine face. I was like, Toddy, I need to see your bride-to-be right now. Why in heaven's name isn't she here with you? He told me you got sick. Do you think it could be morning sickness? I mean, it's technically not morning still, but no matter; babies don't know the difference between morning and night. You could still be pregnant with my grandbaby, and that would be simply wonderful, no incredible, I tell ya. I would be beside myself with joy. Of course, we might need to push the wedding date up a smidge, but that's just fine. You two have waited too long to tie the knot, anyway. If you're not pregnant, you'd better get to working on it. Girls your age start having issues with having babies."

Elaina shook her head. "I don't think I'm pregnant, and I'm only 29. Don't worry; we both want to have kids, just not right this minute. I'm up for a huge promotion at work, and Todd is going to be traveling for work a lot."

"If you're not pregnant, why didn't you come to the airport to pick us up?"

"I thought I was going to throw up. I must have a little virus or something strange going on, but I promise it's not a baby. We're beyond careful in that department."

"Well, don't be careful for too long; this Nana doesn't want to wait too much longer for a house full of little ones." *Ah–the truth finally comes out.*

Todd pulled at his shirt collar and cleared his throat. "Can you go grab that coffee now, babe?"

Shoot! I was too self-absorbed to make the damn coffee! Elaina rose gingerly to her feet, never so glad for an excuse to escape a conversation with Todd's mom. She knew that Jacqueline meant well, but that didn't decrease the pressure to be perceived as the perfect daughter-in-law. *Sigh.* As the coffee brewed, she pulled gingerbread cookies out of a plastic container and placed them on a pewter tray.

When she returned with the coffee, Todd and Thomas stood simultaneously to grab the wobbling silver tray out of her hands. "Thank you. Help yourselves." She gestured toward the cookies.

Thomas leaned in toward Elaina. "So, Todd tells us you're doing exceptionally well at the bank, might even get promoted to vice president this year. That's pretty damn impressive for someone who isn't even 30 years old. I'm mighty proud of you, young lady. You've got quite the career ahead of you."

Flashing him a smile, she mulled over her words momentarily. Ordinarily, Elaina's father-in-law didn't intimidate her. But Thomas had worked as a C-level executive for the past 25 years of his career. A simple, "Thanks, Dad, let's throw one back," wouldn't suffice. "I appreciate that, especially coming from someone with your business acumen and expertise."

The sentiment must have struck the right chord. Thomas dabbed at the corner of his eye with a white embroidered handkerchief and pulled a silver cigar case from the interior pocket of his navy sport coat. "I bought these at the airport so that we could celebrate together at the right moment."

Jacqueline snatched the case out of her husband's hand and huffed. "What on God's green earth are you doin'? This is our elegant future daughter-in-law we're congratulating, not one of your golf buddies who you drink beer with on the ninth hole. Besides, she might be carrying our unborn grandchild." Elaina grimaced. *Why are they putting me in the middle of this awkward confrontation?*

Thomas clenched his jaw. "Give it a rest, Jacqueline. Elaina is a grown woman. She told you she isn't pregnant. Furthermore, she can decide if she wants to smoke a cigar or not. What do ya say?" He held a cigar up toward her and grinned.

"No, thanks. I'm still a little green. I want to make it through dinner tonight, but I'll make you a deal. We can smoke them tonight when we get back home. And I've got a 30-year-old bottle of Greene's Black Label scotch that will pair with them perfectly. Sound like a plan?"

Thomas put his arm around her and looked up at Todd. "Son, you've got a good one. She's pretty, smart, successful and knows her audience. Never let her slip through your fingers. Say, Elaina, can you put these somewhere for safekeeping?" He handed the cigar case to her and patted her shoulder.

She smiled, placing the cigars inside her purse. Suddenly,

her stomach rumbled again; clutching it, she ran to the bathroom. *What in the hell is going on with me?* She kneeled, hugging the toilet as her breakfast came up. Light from the window strobed on the wall, and when the room darkened, there was no question–she was blacking out.

3

JULIA CAROLINE
1960

Sliding into her canopy bed, Julia Caroline curled up with the quilt she'd made in home economics class last year. Soon, the pieces of fabric she had patch-worked together would provide warmth in the bed she'd share with James. Her cheeks reddened at the prospect of being in bed with her husband-to-be. Kissing him lit up the darkest of times; his gentle touch made her weak in the knees. Lovemaking was bound to bring forth an electrical storm of epic proportions. She bit her lip, trying to push the thought out of her mind. It wouldn't do to focus on something she couldn't have yet.

Someone tapped on the heavy oak door to her bedroom. "Julia Caroline, I'm bringing in some laundry. I washed your new dress for the Christmas party and some of your under-things." Her mother barged in with an overflowing basket.

"Mama! I was in bed already. Couldn't the laundry have waited?"

"Young lady–I have a house full of children who need my help. If I waited until each of you were ready for me to do my chores, they'd never get done. You'll find out how it goes soon enough."

Julia folded her arms across her chest. "Nope. I will not have children right away. I have too much ambition for all that."

"And what will James say about that? Doesn't he want you to raise a house full of well-behaved babies and have a delicious dinner on the table by 6 o'clock every day?"

"No, ma'am. We've already discussed it. James wants me to go to college, too. He knows I have a higher purpose than being a homemaker. We're going to wait to have children. He'll help me with the housework and cooking. Besides, we can always heat up TV dinners."

Julia's mother frowned. "You modern girls have some funny ideas, but then again, I wish I'd had the opportunity to consider such options when I was younger. The only choices were to get married, spending your days cleaning, cooking and caring for babies or to live a sad spinster existence, staying in your parents' home until they died and, ultimately, living alone. But promise me one thing, don't mention any of this to your daddy. He doesn't need to know. It will just get him worked up."

"Goodnight, Mama." Julia pulled the blue and pink patchwork quilt over her head and squeezed her eyes closed, hoping her mother would get the message.

"Don't you want to try on your new dress? I need to know if it needs alterations before I go to bed. Otherwise, you'll have to wear it as is. I know you won't have time to do it yourself with school tomorrow."

Sighing, Julia Caroline stepped out of bed. "Yes, Mama. I'll do it right now."

"Good girl. I'll be back to take a look after I take your brothers' and sisters' laundry to their rooms."

Stepping into the dress, Julia admired her reflection. She'd have to thank her mother for insisting that she wear a corset for the past few years. The painful training process had narrowed her waist, giving her the perfect hourglass figure. What was it her mother had said? *Oh, yeah,* "No man wants a plain, unshapely wife." Julia had bitten her tongue to avoid an argument, but James wasn't the type to fuss about her appearance. He loved her for who she was. An oceanfront kiss at five had sealed their love story; she'd never cared what another boy thought about her figure, personality, dreams or plans for the future.

A rapping on the window garnered her attention. She turned to see what had made the noise, but nothing was there. Opening the panes, she poked her head outside to take a closer look.

"Psst ... hey, it's me. Quick! Grab a bag and a change of clothes. Let's go!" James was sitting on the widow's walk a few feet away from her second-story bedroom.

"But Mama will be back any minute–"

"Well, silly, that's why we need to hurry! C'mon." He motioned for her to go back into her room.

With her heart in her throat, Julia evaluated what to do. *Cheese and crackers!* Taking a deep breath, she ran over to her wardrobe, grabbing her purse and an overnight bag, throwing in the first two dresses and undergarments she found, along with her hairbrush and shoes. *That will have to do.*

Steadying her hands, she climbed out the window and carefully avoided the strands of Christmas lights along the roofline to join James. "Okay, now what?"

He placed his finger in front of his mouth. Then, he gestured for Julia to follow him to the edge of the roof, where her father had propped his ladder. The couple tiptoed, making their way to almost certain doom. No doubt her mother had noticed she wasn't in bed by now. It was just a matter of time before she discovered the entire escape route.

Julia held her arms out to her side to maintain balance. "Are you sure this is the best idea?"

Without saying a word, he climbed down the ladder and stepped aside to help her as she did the same.

Motioning with his head toward the main drag, he took off running, avoiding the street lamp in the drive. Her bare feet hit the pavement, ripping at the skin on her soles. Why hadn't she bothered to put her shoes on before leaving her room? Maybe she wasn't cut out for this type of last-minute adventure after all. Should she just turn herself in and face the music?

Julia spotted the Corvette just off a side road. She lengthened her stride just a hair to match James'.

"The doors are unlocked. Just jump in, and we'll get outta here!"

Winded, she followed his instructions. Once she was inside, she gently closed the door, turned to throw her bag in the backseat and exhaled loudly.

James stared at her. "Are you sure you're ready for this?"

"There's no turning back now! Let's see what this car can do. Hit it!" As they sped away, she smiled smugly. Somehow, they'd gotten away with it. One of her siblings must have thrown a fit or gotten sick, requiring their mother's help. Whatever the case, this was the real deal. Tomorrow morning, she'd become Mrs. Julia Caroline Mason, wife, student and a woman who wouldn't settle for finding happiness by meeting the status quo.

After clearing her head, Julia had to wonder what had brought on their current situation. "Hey, I thought you wanted to wait until after we graduated to get married."

James grinned. "That was before I heard from the university. They want me to start taking classes right away. I have enough credits to graduate, and my GPA is higher than anyone else's in school. They worked out a deal with Principal Madison. I have to take the necessary tests for graduation, but I don't have to go to high school daily anymore. It's such a relief."

"That's amazing news!" Julia squealed.

"Yup! My scholarship includes housing and a small stipend, as long as I work in the lab in my spare time. And get this–" he paused, beaming. "My wife can live with me in student housing. We'll have an efficiency apartment. You can finish high school and start classes as soon as you graduate."

Julia bounced up and down on the seat. "So, we won't need our parents' help at all, right?"

"That's the plan." James winked at her.

"That's the best thing I've ever heard!" She sat back in her seat and imagined realizing the absolute freedom she'd been awaiting. Writing had always been Julia's passion, and she'd received high marks on her compositions for English class. Now that there wouldn't be a house full of children begging for her help, she'd be able to polish off some of her own dreams and ambitions for once.

Of course, she still had to finish her high school studies. James' deal with the principal was one-of-a-kind. But that was okay. They could get married, live in student housing in Charleston, and she'd just have to commute to Mt. Pleasant for school for a few more months. Their parents were going to freak out about them eloping, but she couldn't worry about that right now.

4

ELAINA
2021

Elaina came to, slumped over the side of the toilet. She shot upright. "What happened?" The strangely vivid dreams had returned, making her feel like she was inside her grandmother's teenage body looking out at a 1960s version of the family home and other various parts of Isle of Palms.

This wasn't like most dreams, where Elaina had watched a movie-like scene unfold before her eyes. Instead, she could also feel the fabric of Granny Mason's dress brush against her skin and smell the salty Atlantic Ocean air. It was almost as if she'd become Julia Caroline for a short time.

Todd crouched beside her. "You scared us! One minute, you were smiling; the next, you were in here throwing up. We tried to move you into a less awkward position, but you wouldn't let go of the side of the sink. You were mumbling under your breath, something about shrimp and a milkshake, while you were out, too. I've never seen anything like it."

"Should I call your doctor?" Jacqueline asked. "Are you on some type of medication that might have knocked you out?"

Elaina shook her head. "I'll make an appointment for

tomorrow, but I think I'm just a little overwhelmed with the holidays and wedding planning. I'm not taking anything other than birth control."

Jacqueline raised her eyebrow. "Have you been taking your pill every day? If not–"

"Mom, leave her alone. Like dad said, now's not the time for all that." He turned to Elaina and offered her his hand. "Are you okay, honey? Should I cancel the party?"

Taking his hand, she stood. "No. I'll be alright. Just give me five minutes to freshen my makeup." She splashed some cool water on her face and gasped at the sight of the circles that darkened her eyes and accentuated her sallow skin. She reapplied some bronzer, blush and tinted lip gloss. *That's a little better.*

Going out was the last thing Elaina wanted to do, but their parents had gone to great lengths to plan a fun engagement party for them, with roughly 125 guests from all corners of the country. With Christmas quickly approaching, everyone had made a special effort to come. She couldn't bow out now; that would disappoint too many people she loved. Returning to the living room, she plastered on a fake smile. "Alright, I'm ready."

"You're sure?" Todd asked. "I'm sorry if I made you feel guilty earlier. If you need to stay home, you can."

She nodded. "I'm positive. I'll be fine. I'll find a cushy spot to chill out in the hotel ballroom."

Todd slipped Elaina's arms into her coat sleeves and kissed her forehead. "I'll bring you whatever you want to eat. You can take it easy and hang out with your sisters."

As Todd drove them to the hotel, cool air from a cracked window stung Elaina's face. Jacqueline had insisted the fresh air would help them all feel refreshed. Elaina knew she meant well, but that didn't mean her controlling sensibilities weren't irritating.

What bothered her the most was how Todd changed from a confident, easy-going man to a little boy when his mom came into town. Soon, this woman would be her mother-in-law, and eventually, the grandmother to her children. She wasn't quite a monster-in-law; it could definitely be worse. But Elaina's patience was wearing thin. How could she coexist with her in peace?

Neither of the other Nelson sisters would have any advice; their mothers-in-law were sweet, helpful people. Brittany's mother-in-law, Judy, babysat while she managed one of Charleston's largest architecture firms. Of course, Blake had especially lucked out with Nancy, who happened to be their grandmother's best friend.

Both Nancy and Granny Mason had passed away, but their spirits remained to help guide the sisters through the paranormal misadventures that seemed to find them every few years or so. Unfortunately, not all spirits were sugar and spice like these two family matriarchs. After Blake's ex-fiancé, Parker, had died, he'd wreaked havoc in their family's lives more than once. Shivering, Elaina rubbed her arms and pushed the thought out of her mind.

As they pulled up to the magnificent stone hotel in downtown Wilmington, she drew a deep breath. Todd pulled under the porte cochere to drop them off, and he turned to Elaina. "I'll be right there; find a place to rest. Everyone can come to you if they want to talk to you tonight." She nodded and began walking toward the lobby. *Time to smile and pretend everything is okay.*

Walking into the ballroom, Elaina scanned the room for a spot to take up residence. Sofas and armchairs surrounded the corner fireplace, where flames flickered, casting a welcoming glow. She made a beeline for the chair closest to the hearth. Melting into its soft cushions, she closed her eyes and sighed.

"You look cozy," said a familiar voice.

She opened her eyes to see Blake's husband, Clint, grinning ear-to-ear. "Hey, when did you guys get here? Where are Blake and Macy?"

"Macy just woke up from her nap, so Blake is helping her get dressed. They'll be down in a minute. We came up earlier today and took Macy to the Fort Fisher Aquarium. She loved it. We'll all have to go back sometime."

"Definitely. Sounds like fun." She grabbed her stomach to soothe a rumble and stifled a groan.

Clint frowned. "You look a little pale. Are you okay?"

"I will be. There's just been a lot going on lately."

"You haven't seen any of our old *friends*, have you?" His brow furrowed. She knew Clint was referring to Parker and his twin sister, Maggie, who had joined Parker for his most recent stint of torturing the Nelson sisters.

"No. Nothing like that. I've had some stomach issues and dizziness. And these random dreams, well, they're just weird. All of my senses are heightened. Have you ever smelled something during a dream?"

"That would be a negative. That sounds pretty damn strange. Have you told your granny or my grandma about those dreams?"

She shook her head. "Not yet. I didn't think they were worth mentioning. Seriously, let's not worry about it tonight. Everyone's here to have fun."

Clint nodded. "Let me know if you need someone to talk to. I'm always here for you."

"Thank you. Look who's coming!" Elaina pointed to Macy, whose dark ringlets had been pulled into pigtails, accented by red ribbons.

The child ran full force toward Elaina and jumped onto her lap. "Auntie 'Laina! You look so pretty."

"So do you, kiddo. You're gorgeous." She kissed her niece's face repeatedly until the adorable child squealed, squirmed out of her arms and twirled around the floor to Blake, who'd just entered the room.

"Mommy! You're here."

Blake patted Macy on the back and gently pushed her

toward Clint. "Yep. Why don't you and Daddy go order us some sweet tea?"

"Okay. Come on, Daddy!" Macy grabbed Clint's hand and dragged him across the room.

Blake laughed. "That girl knows she has him wrapped around her finger. I wouldn't have it any other way. So, are you excited about tonight?"

Elaina forced a smile. "Definitely. It will be nice seeing everyone."

"Uh, oh. What's the matter?" Blake twisted her mouth and chewed her cheek. "Is Jacqueline causing you some grief? I can get her liquored up and have Clint talk her head off about restoring old cars."

Elaina sighed. Her family could read her like a book; there was no use in holding back any longer. While Elaina explained everything she'd experienced over the past few days, she wondered if there could be some truth to what Clint had mentioned. Was there a paranormal component to her episodes? Could a ghost make her sick? How would that work?

"I think you need to talk to Granny and Nancy, just in case. The sooner, the better. We can go to my room and try to call them. And, despite her many, ahem, charms, your mother-in-law is right. I don't think it would hurt to take a pregnancy test either."

"Okay, but the test will have to wait until I can go to the pharmacy."

"Actually, it won't. I have one in my suitcase." Blake blushed and sighed. "Clint and I have been trying to make a brother or sister for Macy."

Elaina grabbed her sister's hand. "How exciting! I can't wait to have another niece or nephew!" Her excitement made her forget the nausea, if only for a minute.

"Well, let's go find out what's going on with you so we can get back to the party. Todd and all of your guests will start missing you if we're gone too long."

Entering Blake's oceanfront hotel room, Elaina gasped as she took in the view from massive windows. Shimmering grayish blue waves rippled onto the sand. The hotel staff had even built sand sculptures to look like snowmen, complete with Hawaiian shirts and straw hats.

"The view is beautiful! Now, I wish we'd booked a room here tonight, too. Maybe I'll ask Todd and his parents if they want to join you guys here for the rest of the weekend."

"Sounds like fun. Let me grab that test for you, and I'll work on getting Granny and Nancy here." Blake walked over to her suitcase and retrieved a slim white box, handing it to Elaina. "I'll have my fingers crossed that you get your wish, whatever that might be. Love you."

"Thanks, sis. Love you, too. Gah–I can't believe I'm getting ready to take a pregnancy test."

Elaina hugged Blake and walked to the bathroom. After taking the test, she placed it on the sink ledge. As she stood up, the room shifted a bit, and she caught herself on the edge of the sink, bumping the test into the pool of water that circled the drain. *Shoot!* There was still a minute left before the test was supposed to be ready.

She pulled it out of the water and looked at the result window. One dark line to indicate the effectiveness of the test had appeared, and alongside it, there was a faint line. Could she be pregnant? If the test hadn't fallen into the water, would the second line be darker–a more definitive positive? Her heart jumped.

At 29, she wouldn't mind having children sooner rather than later, but she'd hoped for at least six months of wedded bliss without the discomfort of morning sickness and unsexy stretch marks plastered across her stomach.

Someone knocking on the door caught her attention. "Hey, are you okay in there?" Blake asked. "Can I come inside?"

Elaina opened the door. "I'm so freaking clumsy. I dropped

the test in the sink. What does this faint line mean?" She handed Blake the inconclusive test stick.

"It means you need to go to the doctor tomorrow for a blood test. At any rate, you being sick and dizzy is enough to warrant that, pregnant or not. Here, take this baggie to put the test in so you can show Todd later. He'll be so excited!"

Elaina placed the baggie inside her purse and grabbed her lip gloss to touch up her pout before returning to the party. "Did you get in touch with Granny?"

"No, not yet. I still wish we had a more direct line to the Other Side. Hopefully, they'll make it to the party. If not, we'll try again later."

"Alright, let's go back downstairs." As Elaina turned to walk out the door, the walls began closing in on her. The floor wobbled like a trampoline underneath her feet. "On second thought, I need to sit down." She fell backward onto the bed, closed her eyes and drifted away to another body, time and place.

5

JULIA CAROLINE
1960

As James sped onto the highway, Julia studied his stern facial expression–a clenched jaw and narrowed eyes. There had to be more to his story. Why was he keeping it from her?

"What really happened at your house tonight? Why did you decide to get married now?" She rubbed his arm and leaned on his shoulder.

James grunted and slapped the steering wheel. "I wasn't going to say anything, but my dad and I got into a huge fight. He doesn't want me to go to college in Charleston. The old man thinks I should finish high school and go to an Ivy League school this fall. Seriously, he has so many antiquated ideas about the way a man should be educated. And he's going to try to control our lives if we stay around."

"My mother accused me of not being a proper lady because I want to have a career after college instead of being a baby-making machine from day one of our marriage. Geez, parents need to stop being so square and step into the current century. Well, we're going to prove them all wrong!"

"You're right!" Grinning, James put his arm around her.

"Let's crank up some good music, and we'll be in Charlotte before you know it."

Dancing along with the radio, the three-hour drive flew by at record speed. After exiting the highway, James drove through a tree-lined residential area, eventually pulling into the driveway of a beautiful stately home with Corinthian columns and sweeping verandas.

Julia yawned and stretched. "Where are we?"

"This is the inn where my cousin stayed for his wedding night. His wife liked it. I figured it would work for us, too." James winked.

"Hey, we're not married yet, so don't get any ideas. I'm putting my foot down on that. A woman's virtue is a gift for her husband. And that's that." Julia folded her arms across her chest.

"Whoa, before you lecture me anymore, I booked us separate rooms for tonight. You'll be staying in the honeymoon suite tonight, and I'll join you there tomorrow."

Julia blushed and smacked James on the shoulder. "You could have started with that part."

"And miss you turning twenty shades of red? I don't think so. Let's go check-in. I want to get married first thing tomorrow so we can take full advantage of that suite."

"You're really trying to make me blush now, Mr. Mason. That's enough bedroom talk for one night. Thank you very much."

James grabbed their bags out of the car and followed Julia into the inn. After checking in, she kissed James goodnight and went to find her suite. She opened the door to see a vast room with floor-to-ceiling windows, a large bed covered in plush bedding, two elegant armchairs and a writing desk. A pair of French doors led to a living area, where a raging fire crackled in the fireplace. A spruce swag and red knit stockings accented the mantle.

This romantic room would make the perfect place for

James and her to consummate their marriage. A warmth pulsated throughout her body, bringing forth an inward glow. She'd never been more in love with James; their life together was about to begin. How would she be able to sleep tonight?

Julia walked to the en suite bathroom and poured a warm bubble bath. Climbing into the oversized clawfoot tub, she tried emptying her mind and relaxing her body. *Ah! Much better!* After soaking for a few minutes, she caught herself drifting off, so she climbed out carefully and dried her body with a fluffy white towel.

Walking over to the bed, she did something she'd never dared to do in her parents' house. She slipped into bed without even her undergarments, allowing the silky sheets and chenille blanket to caress her skin. *Heaven!* The only thing better would come tomorrow when James joined her here.

She said a prayer, asking God to bless their marriage and careers. This brought her the peace she needed to fall asleep, and she drifted off to dreamland, filled with visions of dancing with her husband, a cute house with a white picket fence and three beautiful children with dark curls.

The later the night grew, the more vivid her dreams. Suddenly, the tone changed from upbeat and happy to guilt-ridden and frustrating. Instead of sweet moments for the new couple, she saw her mother crying in the kitchen at James' house.

Julia woke, her heart aching. In all the excitement, she'd forgotten about their parents and what they might be thinking. Were they really together, trying to find their children? Maybe they should return home and call off the wedding until Julia graduated in the spring. What was their hurry? Wasn't forever worth waiting for?

She pulled on her clothing and dialed James' room. Despite being fully dressed, she was still shivering, so she slipped on a cardigan.

"Aaah, hello?" James yawned.

"Hey, it's me. I think we need to go back home. You know I love you, but this isn't the right time to do this. I have a horrible feeling."

"It's probably just cold feet. Think it over tonight and try to get some rest. We can always drive home in the morning if that's what you want. Okay?"

"Okay," she said, curled up in the bed linens. The sound of someone entering the room startled her. "James? Are you still there?"

"Yep. I'm here, but I want to get some more shut-eye. Either way, we're going to have a big day ahead of us."

"Someone just came into my room," she whispered.

"I'll be right there! Don't do anything crazy." The handset clanged as he hung up.

Jumping up out of bed, she was relieved she'd already gotten dressed. It was probably a hotel maid dropping off some fresh towels, but she couldn't wait for James to get there to confirm the intruder's identity. She untwisted the solid mahogany finial from the foot of the bed, ready to attack. All of those years of playing baseball with her brothers and learning how to knock the wind out of someone with one swift, direct pitch were about to pay off.

Julia crept into the living room, where a dark figure stood. "James? Is that you?" She stared, but there wasn't enough light to distinguish facial features. It was a tall man with a familiar athletic stature. Who could it be, and what did he want?

The man turned toward the window. Illuminated by the moon, the intruder's identity was no longer a mystery. "Mr. Mason? What are you doing here?" Julia's shoulders relaxed slightly. Sure, they were in heaps of trouble, but at least it wasn't someone planning to rob her, or worse. *Ugh.* Eventually, their parents would forgive them for sneaking off to elope. She flipped on the light switch, immediately regretting the decision when she saw Jacob Mason's pinched, blood-red face.

"Where is that boy of mine? You must have used your

witchcraft on him. That's the only reason a young man with opportunities would throw away a full scholarship to a prestigious school. It was enough to kill his daddy. Tell me, you devil woman, are you proud? Are you?" He spat the words in her direction.

"Sir, I don't know what you're talking about. James decided he wanted to accept the offer from Palmetto College. Aren't you proud of him and his decision? I know I am. And there's no need to be dramatic. You're standing right here."

Jacob gnashed his teeth. "Does this look normal to you? He punched the wall, and his fist went straight through it." Pulling his hand back out, he locked eyes with her.

She stared in horror, not sure what to say. "Oh, my! There's no need for parlor tricks. James is on his way up here. We'll leave with you and wait until the right time to get married. Let me pull my stuff together." She frantically grabbed her luggage and the handful of items she'd used since they'd arrived at the inn. "Okay. Let's get James. I'm ready."

Her future father-in-law shook his head. "Young lady, you're not listening to me. I'm dead as a doornail, and I should know. I was a doctor, remember? Y'all's little escapade here caused me to have a heart attack; it got me in one shot. I won't let you rest until you break up with my boy. He's too smart, talented to end up with a second-rate education and a two-bit whore like you."

Tears streamed down Julia's cheeks. She'd been raised to respect her elders, especially men, but she forgot her manners and glared at Mr. Mason. "Seems to me you're the one who is ruining James' life. I hate that he's lost his father because he loved you and looked forward to the day when y'all would work together at your family practice. He wanted you to be proud of him, but maybe that was a lost cause. I won't ever give up on him." She ran over to the bed and threw herself on it, crying face down into a pillow.

Someone pounded on the door. "Julia, let me in!" *Good! It*

was James. He would stand up to his father himself. "Julia, my key isn't working."

Jacob must be holding the door closed. Heat rose to her neck and burned her ears; she flipped over and hopped up off the bed, balling her fists. *Where did he go? He must have gone into the bathroom.* She opened the door for James. "You're never going to believe who broke into my room."

"I don't see anyone or any signs of forced entry, Julia. Are you sure someone is really in here?"

She threw her hands into the air. "Yes! Your father broke into my room, threatened me and said I need to break up with you so you'll go to the right college. He even made up some story about how us eloping had killed him. It was nuts!"

James narrowed his eyes. "Where is he now?" *Great! He didn't believe her.*

"In the bathroom, I guess. When he yelled at me, I got quite mad and threw myself on the bed so I wouldn't have to look at him."

"Wait here for a minute. I'm going to give him a piece of my mind right now." James walked back to the bathroom. His face was as white as a sheet when he returned.

Julia chewed her fingernails. "Did he say something ugly to you, too? I'm not surprised. But we can pack up and go home. I just want everything to go back to normal. We'll get married this spring."

James shook his head. "No. He didn't say anything to me. When I walked inside, there wasn't anyone in the bathroom. I splashed some water on my face. When I looked back up, his reflection was there in the mirror next to mine. Now, he's gone again. I don't know what is happening. Are we both losing our minds?"

"I don't know." Julia pulled a loose curl back behind a bobby pin. "Why is he so angry with me? What did I ever do to him?"

James rubbed his forehead. "Don't you see? He sees you as

an obstacle to him getting what he wanted — for me to go to an Ivy League medical school. He wanted me to take over the family practice, but he thought I should earn my place by going to the best school money can buy. His dad made him go through the same thing. My parents can't accept that I don't need to go thousands of miles away to get a proper education."

"Do you think he will try to kill me?" Julia shivered.

"I won't let that happen. Whatever we have to do, we'll put him in his place. I loved my dad, but this horrible spirit isn't who my dad was. Death has transformed him into something terrifying."

6

ELAINA
2021

Elaina woke to a flurry of activity, beeping and the brightness of an unfamiliar room. As Blake's face came into focus, Elaina reached for her sister's hand. "Where am I? I was having another one of those odd dreams. I could feel the blood pulsating through Granny's veins." She shivered, recalling the harrowing events her grandmother had faced during the nightmare.

Blake sat nearby and patted her leg. "You're in the hospital. We're all worried about you. I talked to Todd and Mom, and we all agreed that this is where you needed to be right now." Elaina heard her sister's words, but they made little sense. She had a little dizzy spell and nausea, but nothing that warranted all this fuss.

Elaina struggled to sit up. "Oh, no! What about the party? I need to get back. All the family–"

"Are you crazy? You're randomly passing out, throwing up and feeling dizzy. There's no way you are going back to the party. Just take it easy there, sis. It's all gonna be okay." *Easy enough for you to say. You're not the one missing your engagement party.*

Todd ran into the room with a bouquet of daisies. "Hey, honey. Why didn't you tell me how light-headed you've been?"

Tears stung the corners of Elaina's eyes. "I didn't want to postpone the party or disappoint anyone who had traveled to be here to celebrate with us."

"We all want what's best for you," Todd said, rubbing her hand. "Don't worry. In case you've forgotten, we're going to have a huge party in a few months. Here's a hint, you'll be the one wearing the gorgeous white dress." He winked at her.

Her mother walked into the room. "What am I going to do with you? You were my calm middle child who never had any drama. You girls have left this old woman's heart faint on more than one occasion."

"Sorry, Mom," Elaina muttered, wriggling in bed. "Do the doctors know what's wrong with me?"

Susan Nelson sighed. "Not yet. They're keeping you overnight for observation, and they'll do some tests in the morning. You're going to have to be patient and try to get some rest." She turned to Todd. "Do you want me to stay the night with her since your parents are staying with you tonight?

Todd grabbed Elaina's hand. "What would make you feel the most comfortable?"

"No one needs to stay here with me." She gestured toward the vinyl-covered recliner. "That chair looks so damn uncomfortable. Anyway, it's not like I'm dying. Go on home, and I'll see you guys in the morning."

"Are you sure? My parents can stay at our place without me. I don't want to abandon you." Todd kissed her hand and held it.

Elaina nodded. "Yep. I'm positive. Let's all just get some rest, and things will seem better tomorrow. I'll text you if I need anything." She needed Todd and his parents to leave right away. The time for hunting down her grandmother and Nancy was overdue, and she couldn't very well do that with her future in-laws on her heels.

Her mother stopped at the edge of her bed. "Call me if you need anything. I'll be here early." She kissed Elaina's forehead before she left. The rest of her family said their goodbyes and filed out of the room until only Blake remained. "Clint has Macy under control. I'll help you find Granny." Blake had an incomparable knack for reaching the Other Side. Her gifts had proven to be stronger than those the other Nelson sisters possessed.

Blake sat down and closed her eyes. "Granny Mason and Nancy, we need you! Elaina is sick, and we're at a loss for what's wrong. Please come to us as soon as you can."

While they waited for their otherworldly guests, Elaina reflected on the day's events. "When I woke up this morning, I didn't expect today to turn out this way. You and Brittany have been through more than your share of craziness. I guess it was my turn."

"You know we'll have your back 100 percent, just like you've always had ours," Blake said. "Now, let's talk about something else until—"

Granny Mason and Nancy appeared in a silvery mist, covered in snow, which began dripping and puddling near the IV drip machine. Elaina shook her head. *Typical Granny and Nancy antics.*

"We're here, girls. Sorry it took us a bit. We got caught in a snowball fight in Iceland. I've always wanted to see the Northern Lights, so we thought we'd take the opportunity. We didn't know that there would be a bunch of teenagers out tonight. Of course, they couldn't see us, but we got caught in the crossfire, and well, they got us good." Granny Mason laughed.

Nancy shrugged her shoulders and rolled her eyes. "Julia Caroline wouldn't let me mess with them. I had the perfect plan to make some kids wet their pants."

"Nancy, the girls called us here for a reason. Let's focus on that." Julia Caroline Mason could be a stickler for staying on topic. "Elaina, why are you in the hospital? I'm guessing it has something to do with why we're here."

Elaina nodded. "I've been throwing up, feeling dizzy and having strange, very realistic dreams. You and Papa are in a lot of them, and you're really young. I don't always remember all the details when I wake up, but I think you were running away together in the last one."

Julia Caroline bit her lip. "Do you think you might be pregnant?"

"Maybe. Do you think that's all that's wrong?" Elaina stared at her grandmother. "Obviously, I've heard of women having morning sickness and slight dizziness, but this seems like so much more."

"No. I don't think that's all, but if you are, it may explain something else. When will the doctors do another pregnancy test?"

"The doctors are supposed to do a bunch of tests tomorrow morning. They didn't mention a pregnancy test, but I'm going to ask for one."

"Has anything else changed? Did you start wearing one of my watches, or what about a ring? I know you're getting married soon. Did your mom give you one of my rings?"

Elaina shook her head. "No. I haven't been wearing any jewelry. My fingers and wrists have been too swollen and puffy. I assumed it was something to do with me being sick, but, to be honest, I hadn't thought much about it." She thought back over the past week, trying to remember anything that had recently changed in her life.

The thin white strap of her purse caught her eye, and she sat upright in bed. She pointed toward the door. "Granny, I've been carrying your black and white purse. Mom gave it to me a few weeks ago. She was cleaning out her closet and asked me if I wanted a few of her bags. This one was hanging beside them, and I asked her if I could have it. I remembered you carrying it when I was a little girl. It looked beautiful with every outfit you wore. I always admired it."

"The purse could be part of the problem, especially if you're pregnant with twins. You know how twins amplify the power around everything," Julia Caroline said. "I've known other pregnant women who have seen a dead person's memories when they used an object that belonged to that person. Imagine what you could do with that blessing if you could learn to harness all of your power. You girls are already incredibly gifted, but this would take the cake."

Nancy winked at Elaina. "I'm the middle child in my family, too. I know how it feels for the attention to be on everyone else instead of me. Just wait and see, though. It sounds like you're going to turn out to have the most useful gift in the family. Kudos, kiddo."

"What do you mean? What makes me so special?"

"You already know that you and your sisters can communicate with the dead, but it seems that you have another ability–seeing the past of the deceased. This will be handy for all of you with the shenanigans that y'all seem to get into."

Granny Mason moved closer to the bed. "She's right. And if your case is like most we've seen, it won't be just my past that you can see. You can visit the memories of anyone who you knew before they died. All you need is one of their earthly possessions."

"But I'm not done learning about your story yet. I'm intrigued."

"Well, dear, enjoy the ride!" Her grandmother handed her the black and white bag and smiled.

Opening the purse, Elaina braced herself for the darkness. As she exhaled, the anticipated void crept over her, and she waited to be submerged into her grandmother's past.

7

JULIA CAROLINE

1960

W hat had they just experienced? Was Julia's future father-in-law really dead? Did his spirit threaten her, or was she hallucinating? The spiritual world wasn't in her wheelhouse; life as a well-bred Southern girl hadn't prepared her for this moment.

Anytime she'd mentioned ghosts or the supernatural, her mother had made the same comment. "The only ghost we talk about in this house is the Holy Ghost. Ladies don't talk about such things. What would the pastor say?" Julia had pushed the possibility of the existence of paranormal beings out of her mind.

James sat down on the bed and hugged his knees to his chest. "I need to call my mother, but I can't bring myself to do it." His lips trembled as the words left them, and a tear streamed down his cheek. "The last thing I said to my dad is that I didn't need him to make my decisions for me anymore. I feel terrible. I can't believe he's gone."

They were too young to lose their parents. James' father dying of a heart attack was especially shocking, considering his lengthy medical background. If their roles were reversed and one of her parents had died, it would still seem unfair. After all, their parents were only in their early 40s and the very picture of health.

Unsure what to say, Julia took his hand. "I'm so sorry, honey. I'll be right here with you, no matter what." He leaned his head against her shoulder and sobbed uncontrollably.

Rubbing his head, she thought through what they needed to do next. "Do you want me to call your mother? I can't imagine how scared you are to talk to her. You have to be feeling so many emotions, and we don't know for absolute certain that your dad is dead. Maybe we saw something unexplainable. One of us should call and find out what's going on for sure."

James wiped his eyes and nodded without saying a word.

Julia rubbed his arm before dialing the operator and asked for the Mason residence. The line rang once, twice, three times. Finally, someone picked up the phone. "Hello?" It was James' mother whose voice, understandably, sounded strained.

"Mrs. Mason, it's Julia Caroline–"

His mother interrupted abruptly, "Is James with you? I need to talk to him immediately."

"Yes, ma'am." She pulled the phone away from her ear, covering the mouthpiece. "Your mom wants to talk to you. Are you up to it? Do you want me to take a message for you?"

James' lip quivered, and Julia's heart sank. "No. I'll talk to her." He took the phone from her, squeezing his eyes shut before he spoke. "Hello, Mama. Yes. I'm sitting down."

He shot up off the bed and paced the floor, stretching the spiral phone cord to its limits. "Oh, God! What happened? Are you alone at home? Can you call Aunt Sandy to come to sit with you until I get home? Yes, ma'am, I understand. I'll be there in the morning to help you take care of things." He rubbed his temples and shook his head. "No, ma'am; we haven't yet. We were supposed to get married in the morning, but Mama, I'm sorry; yes, ma'am."

Listening to James' side of their conversation created knots in Julia's stomach. She was relieved she didn't have to hear his mother's scolding tone. It was clear Mrs. Mason was disappointed in their actions. When Julia considered his mother's perspective, she didn't blame her for being angry. Losing your husband at an early age had to be difficult, but even worse, she knew the stress of their favored son eloping had caused the heart attack. There was no coming back from that moment. If you blame your son and future daughter-in-law for your husband's death, how could you forgive them? Would she ever find it in her heart to do so?

"Goodnight, Mama." James hung up the receiver and fell back on the bed, staring at the ceiling. "I'm going to sleep here tonight, but you don't have to worry about me compromising your virtue. I just don't want to sleep alone tonight." His sobbing shook the bed, and Julia curled up against him, caressing his face.

"You don't have to go anywhere. I told you–I'm here for you, whatever you need. My virtue belongs to you, and you'll receive it when we're legally married. Until then, I will comfort you in any other way I can."

James fell asleep, curled in a ball and pressed up against her body. Her heart ached for this man whom she loved. What could she do to help him heal from his grief? There would be a long road ahead; was listening to him vent enough? Could she do something more proactive? She was confident they'd navigate through the pain together.

Relaxing ever so slightly, Julia began drifting off to sleep. She stirred, tossing and turning for most of the night. After a few hours, a loud bang echoed from the living room. She gently rose out of bed to not disturb James and tiptoed into the other room to turn on the overhead light. After her eyes adjusted, she saw Mr. Mason perched on the sofa. She gasped but held in her scream. James did not need to see his father's spirit again tonight. Shaking, Julia drew a deep breath and stared at the apparition, hoping he would vanish on his own, never to return.

"Having a restful night?" he asked. "I hope so because you took away my peace the day my son realized he was in love with you. I could see the look in his eyes, and I knew he would throw away his chances to go to a great school, all just to marry you. If you kids had just waited to get married until he graduated from medical school, we would have thrown you the wedding of a lifetime. Was it worth killing me, just to get married five years earlier than planned?"

"That wasn't our intention. We're meant to be together, and it's time for us to get married. Wherever James goes, I'll follow and support him wholeheartedly. But I'll be attending college, too. I have my own dreams and career ambitions. Why should it be a problem for us to be married while we complete our coursework? I won't let marriage interfere with our education. I don't know why you died, but you shouldn't blame James. No one should. He loved you and wanted you to be proud of him. He's hurting right now."

Mr. Mason rose from the sofa. "If you truly care about my son's happiness and success, you'll tell him to go away and forget your plan to stay in Charleston. And you need to wait to get married. Tell him it's what you want. It's the only way he'll go along with it."

"Respectfully, sir, it's not what I want." Julia balled her fists by her side. Trembling, she held her head in the air, refusing to break eye contact with him.

"Damn it! I'm telling you to do these things, not asking. You will do as I say. If you don't, I will haunt you for the rest of your blasted life. You will see me in the mirror when you brush your hair, in your soup bowl while you eat lunch, in the reflection of James' sunglasses at the beach and during each of your dreams. I will not relent until you lead him in the right direction. Long story short, I will ruin your life. I don't think that's what you want, child."

Julia answered through clenched teeth. "We're not children any longer, and I was never your child. You can't tell me what to do. I've tried playing nice with you here, and I'm done. I would give my life for that man. Yes. He is a fully grown man. Ultimately, it's his choice where we live, and he's already made his decision." She shrugged and rolled her eyes. "Anyway, there isn't anything you can do about it now that you're dead."

He sneered. "Want to bet?" As he vanished into a silvery cloud, she frowned. There had to be a way to prevent the torture Mr. Mason had promised to deliver. But who could help, and what on earth could they do?

Julia recalled stories her paternal grandmother had shared about unsettled spirits and the superstitions that surrounded them. She'd made the mistake of sharing her grandmother's stories with her mother, who had called the elderly woman a witch and forbidden her to visit with her unsupervised. But maybe it wasn't just a bunch of hocus pocus.

8

ELAINA

2021

When Elaina expected the transition from the present day into the depths of Granny Mason's memories, her experience was much less frightening. However, this most recent journey had taken much longer than anticipated. After being away, she woke up to a nurse fussing with an IV drip.

"Good morning, darlin." The nurse rubbed a bandage onto Elaina's arm over the IV port. "Don't worry. This is just to replenish the fluids you've lost and keep the nausea at bay. It's all totally safe, even if you're pregnant."

Blake walked into the room, carrying two iced coffees. "Is it okay if she has this? It's decaf."

"If y'all can wait until after I do her blood work, it should be fine." The nurse winked. "I'll be right back. We're going to do a pregnancy test and a couple of other blood tests."

"Well, at least you'll know for sure now." Blake's eyes sparkled as she added, "Is it selfish that I hope it's positive? I'd love for us to be pregnant at the same time, and then, our kids could grow up together."

"That would be great," Elaina admitted, despite her initial

hesitation to get pregnant before her first wedding anniversary. Blake lived about three hours away in the carriage house at their family homestead, next door to the main house where she ran a successful bed and breakfast.

Their parents had all but moved in with Blake, only leaving when Susan had to check in on her thriving boutique in Knoxville. Brittany and her family lived about 10 minutes away in a cute house on the marsh in Mount Pleasant.

Maybe eventually, Elaina and Todd could find jobs in Charleston and move closer to the rest of the family. It would be wonderful for everyone to live within 30 minutes of each other. The Nelson sisters' children could grow up together, surrounded by the people who loved them more than life itself. Plus, there would be so many great options for built-in babysitters. No doubt about it, family support would be necessary if she was pregnant. Smiling ear-to-ear, Elaina couldn't stop her inward glow. *Where did that nurse go?*

As if on cue, the nurse walked into the room with a tray filled with empty test tubes. "Okay, hon, hopefully, this will go fast." She wrapped a tourniquet around Elaina's arm and began drawing blood. After filling the vials, the nurse placed a bandage over the withdrawal site. "You handled it like a champ. I'll run these to the lab, and someone from neurology will come to pick you up for a CT scan in a few minutes."

Elaina reached her arms outward. "Wait–when will I know the results, at least for the pregnancy test? I don't know how much longer I can wait!"

The nurse smiled. "Sorry. The lab has been backed up the past couple of days. I promise to come to talk to you after you get back from your scan. Try to stay calm. You have to hold still for the machine. I know it's gonna be hard, but clear your mind as much as you can."

As the nurse walked out of the room, Elaina sighed. In less than an hour, her future would be much clearer, or at least she'd have a sneak peek into what it could be. Sure, a baby would complicate things in her career and put a damper on the romance early in their marriage, but babies were a gift, full of promise and potential.

She'd looked forward to being a mom her entire life, and throughout their relationship, Todd had expressed his excitement about having children whenever the time came. Even if the timing wasn't perfect, the child would be the light of their lives.

"Ahem, excuse me, Ms. Nelson, are you ready to go to Imaging?" A woman in a lab coat stood behind a wheelchair in the doorway.

Shaking herself out of the trance, Elaina nodded. The woman helped her out of the bed and into the wheelchair.

Blake followed them out of the room. "Hey, I'm gonna run by the hotel to check on Macy, but I'll be back soon, and I'll try to smuggle some real food in with me."

A cool breeze brushed against Elaina's arms as they passed through the maze of connecting hospital hallways and eventually stopped at a set of double doors labeled with safety and warning signs about radiation levels. *Was this safe for a potentially pregnant woman?* The lab-coat-clad woman scanned her badge at the security pad, and the doors swung open to a bleak, dark room filled with large medical equipment.

Shivering, Elaina followed the technician's directions, lying on the narrow table but immediately sat up. "Ma'am, should I be concerned about the radiation since I may be pregnant?"

The woman smiled. "Since we're only scanning your head, you should be fine, but we'll put a protective apron on you, just in case." Afterward, the woman placed headphones on her ears and told her to concentrate on the music playing; the test would be over before she knew it.

Calming ever so slightly, Elaina thought back to the nurse's directions to hold still. *I don't want to have to go through this coffin-like machine more than once!*

The woman left the room. Moments later, she spoke to

Elaina over an intercom, letting her know the scan was about to begin. Elaina closed her eyes and relaxed her muscles as much as she could. Thoughts about holding a sweet, cooing baby with dark curls occupied her mind, helping her find comfort even during the machine's constant booming and banging sounds. If the pregnancy test came back negative, she and Todd could always reexamine their plans to wait a year to try to conceive.

After the test ended, the woman helped Elaina back to her now empty room. And Elaina carefully climbed into her bed, covering herself with a weighted hospital blanket. *Blake must have left.* Yawning, she decided to take a nap. Warm and comforting sensations filled her body as she dreamed of the beautiful baby she imagined during the CT scan. It was a dream she never wanted to leave, confirming her genuine desire to be a mother sooner rather than later.

She woke to a kiss on the cheek from Todd. "Hey, when did you get here? Where are your mom and dad?"

"About an hour ago. I asked them to stay at our place this morning so we could have some time alone." He smiled. "I didn't want to wake you, but the nurse just came by to give you your test results. She said she'd be right back if I wanted to try to wake you up."

Elaina sat straight up in bed. "Oh, my God. What do you think she's going to say? What if I'm pregnant? What if I'm not? What if there's something wrong with me?"

"Whatever she says, we'll figure it out as we go." He picked up her hand and kissed it. "Your face is a little flushed. Don't forget to breathe, honey."

He's so sweet. But regardless of his sentiments, Elaina's heart raced. No amount of deep breathing was going to help calm her at this moment. She sipped some water from the insulated cup on her bedside table, clutching it so hard her knuckles turned white.

The nurse walked into the room, chuckling. "My, whatever did that poor cup do to you? Remind me to stay on your good side. I'm guessing your nerves are all over the place right now, so I'll get straight to the news you're waiting for. Is it okay if he's in the room?" She gestured toward Todd.

"Yes. We're engaged, so you can say anything in front of him."

The nurse smiled. "The pregnancy test came back positive, and the pregnancy hormone levels were much higher than normal."

Todd jumped up. "So, what does that mean? Is Elaina okay? Is there anything wrong with the baby?"

"This most likely means one of two things–either she's much further along than you expected, or there are multiple babies. Do twins run in either of your families?"

Elaina and Todd both shook their heads.

The nurse checked off a few things on the clipboard attached to the door. Standing in the doorway, she smiled. "Well, don't worry about a thing. I'll be back to check on you later. It looks like your mom is headed in here, so I'm going to leave so you can share the good news."

Susan entered the room just as the nurse left. "What's the good news?"

Elaina and Todd shared the surprising information they'd just received and smiled at each other. Having children would be a new adventure, but a welcome one.

Susan's eyes glistened as she leaned in to hug each of them. "I can't tell you how excited I am to be a grandma again! Now, all of my girls will be moms to some fortunate kids! We're all so blessed."

"We truly are. I can't wait to meet these babies!" Elaina's heart leaped. Life had a funny way of changing when you least expected it.

After a few minutes of chatting about possible baby names and nursery color schemes, Todd rose and made his way to the door. "I'll let you guys talk. I'm going to grab us some coffee. Do you need anything else?"

"No, thanks, sweetie. See you soon." Elaina watched Todd leave the room and gasped as a silvery mist glowed over her bed.

"What's wrong?"

"I thought a spirit was about to appear, well, in bed with me, which would have been odd even for Granny or Nancy."

Susan sighed. "I've always thought of the gift to see and communicate with ghosts as a curse. But I have to admit that I feel helpless when you girls are fighting against an evil spirit. Of course, I'd love to see Mom and Nancy again. I miss both of them so much." She dabbed her eyes with a tissue.

Elaina grabbed her hand. "Mom, you don't have to worry about us. We've got each other's backs and yours, too. And it's not like we have a lot of casual conversations with Granny Mason and Nancy. Usually, when they're around, they're helping us out of a bad situation."

The silver film shimmered again, and Granny Mason appeared, crashing into the over-bed table, where Elaina's uneaten breakfast sat.

Susan jumped at the sight of dishes clanging onto the floor, seemingly on their own. "Um, Elaina, do you see someone? Is it my mom?"

"Yep. Granny, what is going on with you today? Is something wrong?"

"Child, I've tried to hide this from you girls. But ever since I died, I've been trying to go back and forth between the edge of Heaven's Gate and the Great In Between, the place you go when you die before you fully cross over to the Other Side. I wanted to watch over y'all but still get to see Papa. My spirit is growing weary, though. It is stretched too thin. Just before Parker haunted poor Blake, I had decided to cross over to

Heaven for good, but then, I saw that you girls needed me more than ever. But now that you've developed this new gift, I feel like it's my time to move on to my final resting place. You'll be able to dip into my memories anytime you need some help. Nancy plans to stay around. Most of her loved ones are still earthbound; she wants to help protect you all."

Elaina shook her head. "Granny, we don't want to lose you! Don't you want to meet my babies?"

"Papa and I will always shine down on you from Heaven. I know you're going to be a great mother. Don't worry. I'll say my goodbyes to the rest of the family."

Susan scrunched up her face. "Is she going somewhere? Mama?"

"She has to cross over to Heaven," Elaina cried. "It's time for her to go to Papa for good." Tears rolled down her cheeks, dampening the collar of her hospital gown.

Susan reached out into the air. "Mama, I wish I could see you one more time, but I'll settle for a hug," Susan said. "I love you. Hug Daddy for me, too."

Granny Mason leaned in to hug Susan. She kissed Elaina's forehead and stared at her. "I love you both. This isn't bye forever. I'll see you on the Other Side."

Elaina's heart ached. They had just gotten their grandmother back six years ago, when Blake's ex-fiancé, Parker, died. His haunting had challenged their family. Without their grandmother's and Nancy's guidance, they wouldn't have figured out how to banish him from their lives. Not only that, but Granny Mason's presence, both during her life and after her death, had been a source of comfort for the Nelson sisters.

As Elaina shifted to pick up a water bottle off the table, something cold slid down her neck and the front of her hospital gown. She jumped up out of bed, squirming in place and shaking her gown. "Ew! What was that?" A tarnished silver locket and coiled chain lay on the floor.

"That's my mom's locket," Susan said. "She always said it

49

protected her, but I never thought about what she meant by that."

Picking up the necklace, Elaina examined the detailed scrollwork, flanked by two lightning bugs at each corner. The clasp gave a satisfying twist, opening to showcase a black and white photo of Papa on one side and her Granny's stunning senior picture on the other. A ray of light blinded Elaina, catching her off guard. "Mom, Blake, anyone?"

No one answered. The light spiraled, floating out of the window. And, then, there was only darkness.

9

JULIA CAROLINE
1960

Clutching her overnight bag, Julia walked outside to the car and waited for James to take their room keys to the lobby. She didn't want to return to the island without getting married, but what else could they do under these circumstances? His father had just died. As frightening as the haunting had been, there were far more challenging events about to take place in their households. Would their parents ever forgive them?

James opened the front door and stepped outside, locking eyes with Julia. His frown and weary eyes broke her heart. She sighed. *Today is going to be loads of fun.* When he sat down in the driver's seat, he broke down crying.

"I don't think I can face my mom. She definitely blames me for my dad's heart attack. I know it isn't true. There had to be something else going on with him, but I can't think of anything to help her see that or make the situation better."

Julia leaned on James' shoulder, playing nervously with the locket he'd given her last Christmas. "I'm so sorry, honey. I'm not sure what to do either, but I'm here for you whatever you decide."

James turned to her. "I want to get married."

"Now? But what about your mom and your sisters?" Julia raised her eyebrows.

"I've never been more sure of anything in my life. We're in this together, and I can take you back home as my wife just as easily as my fiancé. Let's go to city hall before we drive back home."

He put the car into drive, but instead of turning right to drive toward downtown, the car sped toward the highway. James stared down at his hands, shaking his head.

Julia gasped. "What are you doing? Did you change your mind? You don't have to drive so fast; slow down!"

"I'm not doing anything! It's like the car has a mind of its own. Look!" He removed his hands from the steering wheel and his foot from the accelerator, but the car continued driving.

"How on earth are you doing that? This is no time to be joking around."

"Seriously! I have no control over the car now. It's as if the car is driving itself."

She grabbed him by the shoulder. "Pull over now! You're scaring me to death. I don't know why you're doing this, but I don't want anything to do with it. I'll call one of my girlfriends to come to pick me up." What was James thinking? He occasionally made light-hearted jokes but had never pulled a stunt like this.

"I'd love nothing more than to pull over, but I can't," James said, his voice shaking. "I don't know what to do."

A disembodied laugh roared through the car. "Don't worry, kids. I've got this situation under control. You actually thought you were going to get away with your little scheme to elope. Apparently, you don't know me very well."

Julia shrieked, jiggling the handle to the car door to jump out even though the vehicle was rolling at a fast clip. *I'd rather take my chances of not surviving than stay in a car driven by a ghost who hates me!* Despite her efforts, the door didn't budge. She pressed her head firmly against the seat, breathing deeply, trying to calm herself. Stories of car crashes and explosions crept into her mind. Her stomach rumbled, and the bottom fell out. "Oh, no! I'm going to throw up!" Rummaging around on the floorboard, she found a paper sack and heaved into it twice.

James took his eyes off the road and winced. "Ugh, I think Mama put some peppermints in my glove box."

After mashing the glove box button, the door flipped open. Sure enough, there were ten red and white candies inside a small bag, along with a note, "Hope you feel better. Love, Mom." Mrs. Mason must have put the candies into the glove box in case James got an upset stomach while driving. Even in this frightening moment, the simple gesture tugged at Julia's heartstrings. She'd never seen Mrs. Mason as the thoughtful type. Mostly, her future mother-in-law devoted her time planning galas with the women's society club.

Maybe the socialite had more maternal substance than met the eye. If so, she must be beside herself at this very moment. The heavy presence of regret found its way into the pit of Julia's stomach. Not only had Mrs. Mason's husband of 20 years passed away, but their eldest son had betrayed their trust, leading to the stress that had caused Mr. Mason's heart attack.

Julia's thoughts turned to her own mother, who frequently served her family shrimp and grits with a side of guilt and anguish. Their family had been fortunate, especially financially, but her mother believed in a hands-on approach to raising children. She didn't believe in hiring nannies or babysitters and took the spare the rod, spoil the child philosophy to heart. When Julia returned home, there would be hell to pay in the short term, but soon enough, she'd graduate from high school and marry James.

Suddenly, the car jerked to the right, crossing two lanes of traffic at once, narrowly missing a delivery truck before coming to an abrupt stop on the shoulder. Julia put her hands on the dash to keep from falling over.

James' eyes widened. "Damn it. Are you okay?"

Her lip quivered. "I think so, but what just happened? I can't wrap my head around it." She placed her hands on her temples. "You heard your dad talking, right? Was he really driving the car? How does that work?"

James stared off into the distance and shook his head. "Yeah. I heard him, too. I guess he wanted one more chance to control my destiny. I'm not sure what to think. All I know is I wasn't driving the car. Have you ever seen anything like this in your life?"

"Never," Julia whispered, shrinking into her seat.

"Well, we're about an hour away from home. If we make it there alive, we'll have to face the music."

"Sounds like a gas." Julia crossed her arms and fumed. Her emotions had transformed from shock and terror to anger. How dare their parents steal her and James' happiness. It wasn't about them, after all. If everything had gone according to plan, the should-have-been newlyweds would have been on their way back to the inn to consummate their marriage. They were old enough to make their own decisions. Their parents needed to butt out, or at the very least, offer advice and back off when Julia and James didn't accept it.

The rest of the trip flew by. Before Julia knew it, the Corvette was coasting down the main drag on the island. When James signaled to turn onto Palm Court, Julia's heart sank, and a wave of nausea struck when he parked in her parents' driveway. "Ugh. Do I have to go in there?"

James sighed. "I think you'd rather go in there than go to my house right now. Don't worry, though. I'll smooth things over with my mother in time. I'm still in shock about my dad. It's impossible to accept that my dad will not be sitting in his chair, smoking a pipe, when I walk into the house. He was a good man, just controlling. I know he wanted what was best for our family." His eyes misted momentarily, but he drew a deep breath. "I love you, don't forget that."

Julia opened the car door and climbed out. Her overnight bag seemed to have grown heavier. Maybe it was resisting going inside, too. She walked over to the driver's side door, opened it and bent over to kiss James on the cheek. "I love you. Call me as soon as you can."

He grabbed her by the waist, pulling her closer to him. "I will, sweetheart. I'd better get going, though. Talk to you soon."

Julia leaned against the nearby street lamp and closed her eyes before taking a rejuvenating breath. She marched up the steps and opened the front door, expecting the worst. *Here goes nothin'.*

Her mother sat at the kitchen table, staring at her. "Well, is it done?"

"Is what done?"

"Are you married?" Her mother took a drag off her cigarette.

"Not yet." Julia sighed, playing with her engagement ring. "It was horrible–Mr. Mason passed away. When James called his mother last night, she told him. We came home first thing this morning."

Her mother's eyes widened, and her chest heaved. "Goodness gracious! What happened?"

Julia provided the details she knew, leaving out the part about seeing Mr. Mason's spirit and the other events she couldn't quite explain. Her mother wouldn't believe her, so there was no use reliving those horrific moments.

After a few moments, her mother grimaced. "What about the other thing?"

Julia scrunched up her forehead. "What thing?"

Her mother frowned, and she moved her head to the side. "You know, *that.*"

All the blood from Julia's body filled her hot face. "No, Mama. Only my husband will have that privilege."

"And I trust that will not happen now until you graduate from high school? No daughter of mine will walk the graduation stage carrying a baby, even if she is married. We are not that type of family. You must respect tradition, rules and our religious beliefs. You and James are not to spend time together unsupervised from here on out until you have that diploma in your hand. Do you understand?"

Julia bit her tongue. There was no use in arguing when Mama had made up her mind. She'd loosen up over time, but for now, Julia would lie low.

Her mother put her hands on her hips. "I said, 'Do you understand, young lady?'"

"Yes, ma'am. I understand. Am I still permitted to go to the party tonight? Several of my friends are expecting me to be there to lend a hand."

"Unfortunately, your father paid good money for our tickets, and it's for charity. So, we all have to go and pretend to be happy about it. Otherwise, I'd tell you to sit this one out and consider the stress and pain you two young people have caused. Unless Mrs. Mason and James need you to attend any funeral-related gatherings. Since Mr. Mason has passed away, you need to be attentive and respectful. And one more thing—whatever you do, don't tell anyone about the details around Mr. Mason's passing. No one outside of the family needs to know."

Julia nodded. "I would like to take them dinner before we go to the party. Would you help me make your chicken and broccoli casserole?"

"I think that's a fine idea. Let's get you an apron." Her mother stood, smoothing the wrinkles out of her own apron–a uniform of sorts for the handsome 41-year-old woman who ran their household while Julia's father worked six days a week. She handed Julia a starched white eyelet pinafore and helped her tie the back. "You need to pull your hair back, too. You don't want to feed a clump of hair to poor, grieving Mrs. Mason." Julia twisted her hair, forming it into a bun and securing it with a barrette from her skirt pocket.

Like most Southern cooks, Julia's mother didn't need a recipe to piece together dinner for their family. She went to the refrigerator, pulling fresh vegetables, meat and cream from the shelves. Julia began chopping the vegetables on the patinated butcher block countertops, almost creating a melody that harmonized with the boiling of the water her mother had placed on the stovetop.

They hadn't worked together like this in a long time. Instead, it had seemed like they had been working against each other. Julia made a mental note to make more of an effort to get along with her mother. After she set up her own home with James, she would need her mother's advice for certain situations, especially when the babies came along in the distant future. Had it taken a drastic move like Julia running away to elope for both women to realize how much they needed each other?

10

ELAINA

2021

Coughing, Elaina regained consciousness and steadied her shaking hands on the bed rails. "What just happened? Was it the locket? I saw this bright light, and–" Her arms fell back onto the bed.

"Calm down, honey. The stress isn't good for the babies." Susan rubbed her hand. "Your sisters and I have been talking. We think Granny wanted you to have the locket and the memory you just saw."

"I'm sure that's true, but why didn't she call attention to it when she gave it to me? And why was the experience so different from when I blacked out while holding the purse?"

"I don't know the rules or reasoning, but I know my mom wouldn't do anything that would hurt you. What did you just see?"

Elaina drew a deep breath and shared the details of her experience with her mother. "The transition from consciousness to unconsciousness and back to being awake has been the worst. I don't know if I can bear going through that again."

"Why don't I put the locket inside your purse. You can put it somewhere safe when you get home, just in case you need it.

Lord knows it won't do me any good." Susan made up for her lack of supernatural gifts by providing unconditional support and love to her daughters.

"Works for me." Elaina handed the necklace over to her mom; the Nelson sisters couldn't ask for better. When they were younger, their mom had been preoccupied with running her thriving clothing boutique. She hadn't been able to spend as much time with them as she wanted. When Macy was born, she'd semi-retired, putting her trust in her management staff to keep the day-to-day business under control. Susan's new freedom had given her more time with her daughters and grandchildren.

Todd returned with hot tea for them. "I wasn't sure if coffee, even decaf, was a good idea, but the cafeteria had your favorite tea—Charleston Tea Plantation peach. I asked Ryan, and he thought it would be okay." Brittany's husband, Ryan, worked as an emergency room physician at East Cooper Medical in Mount Pleasant, South Carolina. His medical expertise had come in handy more than once.

"That's so sweet. Thanks." Elaina sipped her tea. "Are Ryan and Brittany still here? I haven't gotten to see them very much."

"Oliver got super cranky and needed a nap, so she's dropping them off at the hotel."

Elaina hugged her arms to her chest. "Aww. I haven't held the little guy in weeks. Brit sent me some pictures of him, and he's growing like a weed. Did I tell you his doctor said he'd be a strong candidate for a cochlear implant after his first birthday?"

Her sister had a degenerative hearing loss disorder, triggered by a high fever when she was a toddler. When Ryan realized seven-month-old Oliver didn't respond to his voice, he called in a favor at the hospital's audiology lab for an emergency hearing test the next day. The happy and otherwise healthy child had been diagnosed with complete hearing loss in one ear and only 15 percent hearing in the other. The pediatric audiologist was unsure of what had caused the hearing impairment since their family didn't have a history of deafness, and Oliver hadn't run a high fever liked Brittany had.

Although Elaina had grown up with a deaf sister, she couldn't imagine what the child might go through at this development stage. His fussiness had upset Brittany many times, which bothered Elaina, too. Was he missing out on developing a sense of security and being soothed by his parents' voices? Her heart hurt for him either way. *Poor, sweet Oliver. We'll help you find yourself and your unique way to take on the world. No one in this family is cookie-cutter, and that's more than okay!*

"What have you guys been up to since I left?" Todd asked, taking a big gulp out of his steaming cup.

Elaina narrowed her eyes at her mother. "Oh, we've just been talking. There's so much we still need to do for the wedding, and y'all know I'm an evangelist for the body positivity movement, but we need to do it quickly before I get too big to walk."

Being on the curvy side, she knew her fate as a pregnant woman, especially considering two babies were on board. "I'll probably have to be on bed rest after the first half of the pregnancy. Most of my friends who've given birth to twins haven't had a choice."

Susan scooted to the edge of her seat. "How about a Christmas wedding at the Mason B&B? Then, we'd have Blake and Clint's anniversary to celebrate at Thanksgiving and yours at Christmas every year. Brittany and Ryan would be the odd ones out with their late June wedding, but we can always throw a party for them on July 4. My daughters–the holiday brides."

Todd grinned. "You put a lot of thought into things like this, don't you?"

"You have no idea!" Elaina laughed.

Susan blushed. "I love my girls, and they've all chosen wonderful men to spend their lives with. And now, all of you will have babies, which thrills me to pieces."

"A December wedding would make sense. What do you

think?" Elaina smiled at Todd. "We only have a month until Christmas. I'm good with getting married around the fireplace in the B&B. It will be warm and cozy, with just the two of us and our immediate family members and a couple of friends. It will save us a bunch of money."

As a banker, Elaina pinched pennies pretty hard. Retiring with a comfortable nest egg was critical. She'd seen too many people reach their 60th birthday and realize they didn't have enough saved for retirement. She refused to let that happen to her or anyone she loved. Now, she had two children's college funds to consider, but she lived well below her means. Todd had recently moved into her condo, agreeing it was silly to throw away money on rent when he could live with her for free. Being dual-income with only one mortgage should make a massive difference as they prepared for their exciting future together.

"That works for me," Todd said. "We'll tell my parents when they stop by later today."

"Have you told them about the babies yet?"

"Nope. I wanted you to be with me when I told them. It's our news, not just mine." His eyes sparkled. Todd could be serious and reserved, but his love for Elaina and their unborn children was more than apparent. He'd make a wonderful father, teaching the children many things that would prepare them for life's hard knocks.

A loud crash came from the hallway. Elaina looked up to see a beautiful lab-coat-clad woman with dark hair picking up a clipboard and pen. Giving Elaina a sheepish grin, she walked into the room.

"Sorry about the noise. I'm Dr. Ramirez. I see congratulations are in order—you're having twins! From what we can tell, you're about 12 weeks along. I'm surprised you're just now having symptoms. At any rate, I'd like you to follow up with your regular OB/GYN this week. They'll give you an approximate due date and the like. Now, I'll cover the rest of your test results. Everything came back great. I heard you've been blacking out and having bouts of dizziness and nausea. Is that correct?"

Elaina frowned but nodded. "Did you pick up something on the scan?"

"Not a single thing. As you know, nausea is common during pregnancy, and some women get lightheaded or dizzy. But just to be sure, I've made an appointment for you to see a neurologist here at the hospital, but we couldn't get you in until after the holidays. In the meantime, I want you to journal about how you are feeling in the morning, afternoon and evening. Don't leave out a detail. That will help us have the bigger picture of what's going on with you. I'll send the nurse back to help you with the discharge paperwork. I think some R&R will do wonders for you, so I want you to go home and rest. No work this week, do you understand?"

"Yes, but–" A million thoughts raced through Elaina's mind. Who would pull the reports she needed for her presentation? Who would put together and deliver the presentation?

"I'm sorry. I know how hard it can be to take off from work for a week, but they'll manage without you. When I had my first daughter, I had to learn that you can't be a superhero all the time. Trust me. Life with kids will be easier on you if you can learn when to ask others for help."

The nurse who'd been so kind to Elaina walked into the room. She'd pulled on a red cardigan with a name tag attached. Her name, "Glenda," seemed to fit her upbeat personality. "Oh, doctor, stop giving this poor girl such a hard time. She'll figure it out, and it looks like she has a great support system." She winked at Elaina and handed Todd the release paperwork. "I'll give you two a few minutes to fill this out, and I'll be back."

Elaina picked up her clothing and went into the bathroom to change. It was a relief to trade the stiff hospital gown for the cozy leggings and oversized sweatshirt Todd had brought her. Sliding on her sneakers, she sighed. With the change in wardrobe and getting rehydrated, this was the most comfortable she'd been in several days.

She walked back into the room, and the nurse gestured toward a wheelchair. "It's hospital policy. Think of it as a little more relaxation before you have to go back home. If your family wants to pull their car around to the front, we can meet them downstairs in just a minute. It's cold, so I don't want to make you have to wait out there too long."

Susan rose from her chair and handed Elaina her purse. "Here you go, sweetie. I'll meet you and Todd at your place. I'm going to stop at the grocery store first to pick up lunch for us. Do you need anything else?"

"No thanks, Mom. See you later."

Todd turned to Elaina. "I'm going to go get the car. I'll see you in a minute, honey." He kissed her cheek and left the room.

The nurse walked around the room and looked over at Elaina. "Do you have all of your belongings? I thought I saw a necklace lying around here somewhere earlier today."

"Yep. I've got everything in my purse. I'm ready to go." The hospital hallways were decked out with tinsel and cute holiday drawings by local elementary school students. As adorable as the drawings and decorations were, she was so ready to get home to lie down on her own bed and binge-watch TV shows like crazy while eating Chinese takeout and ice cream.

"Okay. Let's go."

The nurse passed up the bank of elevators her family had used. "Everyone uses these elevators, and they get backed up. Don't tell anyone, but we can use the staff elevator. It will be so much quicker."

Elaina sat back for the ride as the nurse navigated the hallways to a dark wing of the hospital. A cold draft chilled her, but she couldn't locate the source, not a window in sight. Finally, they arrived at a single elevator in a dimly lit alcove. She scoffed internally. *Is this really the faster, better option? I just want to get home!*

Finally, the elevator arrived on the sixth floor, and Glenda pushed her inside. "Here we go! I know you must be ready to get out of this place."

"Definitely. I'm ready to take a shower, eat a whole pizza and sleep for hours."

"I'm sure that won't be a problem at all, dear."

Elaina winced. *What an odd response!* She was an adult in charge of her own schedule. How could it conceivably be a problem?

When the elevator stopped, Glenda pushed her into what appeared to be part of a parking garage, which was empty except for three vans bearing the hospital logo. Todd's car and the hospital entrance were nowhere in sight.

"Where are we?" Elaina asked. "Please take me to my family immediately."

Glenda didn't respond. Instead, the wheelchair tumbled over, dumping Elaina and her purse onto the rough concrete. "I'm so sorry about that! Are you okay?" Elaina nodded, noticing that the nurse's wide smile, making it clear she wasn't sorry at all. But why would a nurse dump a pregnant woman in a wheelchair onto the concrete?

The nurse offered her hand. "Here, let me help you up. Oh, some things have fallen out of your purse."

Without giving it any thought, Elaina scooped up the open locket with her trembling hands. As the chain passed through her hands into the purse, she fell backward and drifted off to another time, another place.

11

JULIA CAROLINE

1960

S tanding in front of the grand three-story home, Julia gulped. Her future mother-in-law was a hard pill to swallow on the best of days. Dread couldn't even begin to describe how she felt about entering the house, but it was time to grow up and face the music. She knocked delicately on the heavy oak door, and the Masons' housekeeper, Mrs. Gregory, answered the door. She cleared her throat and placed one hand on the door frame. "Miss Julia, the family isn't receiving visitors right now."

"Mrs. Gregory, I've brought my mama's homemade chicken and rice casserole for them."

"You and half of the Lowcountry." The woman, whose hair was more salt than pepper, led her to the kitchen and gestured to the long butcher block countertop where casserole dishes, pie plates, and tureens of every color, shape and size lined the entire surface. "Please set your covered dish over there with the others, and then, you'd best be going. Mrs. Mason has asked for her family not to be bothered tonight. They've suffered a great loss, and it's time for their family to heal."

"But I'm James' betrothed, for goodness' sake!" Julia held

her sparkling engagement ring up as if she were presenting evidence to a jury.

"Yes, ma'am, it's a beautiful ring. I'm truly sorry, but I can't let you see him. I promise to deliver a message directly to him if you'd like."

Julia fumed and bit her lip. She had nearly become James' wife earlier that day and would have if Mr. Mason hadn't cast his spell, possession or whatever he did to foil the young couple's elopement plans that morning. Weren't you supposed to be in control of your destiny at 18? Should your parents still have that much control over your life, especially if they were dead?

Mrs. Gregory handed her a pad of paper and a pen. "Here you go, dear. Please make it quick, though. I need to get back to the laundry."

Scribbling her concerns to James, Julia asked him to come over to her parents' house for breakfast the next day. *They can't keep us apart forever!* After closing the note by sending him her love, she handed the folded paper to Mrs. Gregory and thanked her.

As she walked out the door and crossed the pathway back to Palm Court, she clenched her fists. It was wrong for Mrs. Mason to keep her away from James. She made a vow never to allow that to happen again. *She gets a pass tonight since her husband just died.* But Julia was about to become the most important woman in James' life. He'd made that clear to her on many occasions. *Poor James, how was he feeling right now?*

Obviously, he was sad and overwhelmed. Was his mother allowing him to process his own emotions? Did he have to hold her up? He was a good man and a dependable son. The elopement was out of character for him. His mother likely blamed Julia for the entire ordeal, beginning with stealing her son's heart and ending with Mr. Mason's heart attack. Tomorrow, at breakfast, they'd figure out a plan to escape again when things had calmed down.

Opening the white-picket gate to her parents' expansive garden, she sighed. It was time to get ready for the party, but she wasn't looking forward to going now. Her heart ached for James. She entered the house to see her mother sitting at the kitchen table.

"How was Mrs. Mason taking everything? Is James okay?"

"Mrs. Gregory wouldn't let me see them. She let me write a note for James, but that was it. I was so flustered. I didn't know what to do."

Her mother grabbed her hand. "Hon, it will be okay. I promise. Give their hearts some time to heal. Why, I can't imagine if it had been your daddy who'd died."

"I know. It's just frustrating right now. I asked James to come over for breakfast in the morning in my note. I hope that's okay. We don't have to make anything elaborate. Just toast and coffee will be fine."

"Of course, he's always welcome here as long as you're not alone in the house." Her mother glanced at her watch. "Are you up to going to the party? I know I made a big deal about you going earlier, but if you're not up to it, you're welcome to stay home. I can have one of your sisters help your friends serve the punch, clean up dirty dishes or whatever tasks they've assigned you."

Julia drew a deep breath. "I think that would help, Mama. I'm so exhausted. I'd love nothing more than to pour a hot bath and climb into my bed extra early tonight." She began walking toward the staircase at the edge of the living room but turned back toward her mother. "I'm sorry if I worried you. That wasn't my intent, not even a little."

"I know, dear, but you'll find out one day that a mother always worries about her babies, even when they're practically grown and out of the house. I want what's best for you, and for now, that's finishing high school. After that, you're free to begin your life as an adult, whether that means going to college, getting married or both. I love you, Julia Caroline."

"Love you, too, Mama." She blew her mother a kiss and ran up the steps to her en-suite bathroom.

Turning on the tub faucet opened the floodgates to the emotions she'd been holding inside. She couldn't see through her tears, so she reached out for the wall and gently slid into the bubbling tub. The warm water comforted her a little, and she closed her eyes. This was much better than being at the ostentatious holiday party, where she would have needed to pretend to be happy. There shouldn't be a need for pretending. It was Christmastime, and she was engaged to the love of her life. So much for being full of holiday cheer.

Julia's mother was right. Things would get better again. Next Christmas, she'd be Mrs. Julia Caroline Mason. Couldn't they skip the next six months and start living again during a time of happiness?

After soaking for half an hour, she placed a wrinkled hand on the side of the tub and pulled herself out of the cooling water. Entering her bedroom, she pulled a robe off the hook on the door and slipped it onto her body before collapsing onto her bed. The stars twinkled a radiant gold, calling her to the open window.

"Enchanting, aren't they?" a familiar voice asked.

Julia turned to see Mr. Mason standing at the door to her bedroom. Suppressing a scream, she held her breath and gathered her bearings. After exhaling, she stared at him. "Why are you here? You got what you wanted—we came home without getting married. Aren't you satisfied? James is with your wife, so if you're looking for him, go home."

"I know you're still plotting. You forget that I've known you your entire life. You're a clever girl, and I know you can be stubborn. As a matter of fact, I warned James about this very attribute when he shared his plans to propose to you. I knew this fire you have in you would burn us all one day, and well, here we are. You've got us in a fine spot, a fine spot indeed. I hope you're satisfied with your smug self, young lady."

Julia thrust her hands into the air and let out a deep growl. "I've already apologized to you, and I will make amends to your wife as soon as she begins receiving visitors again. I tried to go see her and James tonight, but Mrs. Gregory sent me packing as soon as I sat my casserole dish down on your countertop."

"Good for Mrs. Gregory. James would be better off if he never spoke to the likes of you again. He doesn't need a wife with ambition. A woman's place is keeping the home in order and raising the children to be respectable adults. Why couldn't you have waited until he graduated from medical school to set up a house? Then, you could have had a home full of children to occupy your time."

Julia put her hands on her hips. "I've made it clear that's not all that I want out of my life. The children will come along after I've finished school and started my career. And they will be respectable members of society, just like James and me."

"Blast it all, girl. You leave me no choice!" He struck her with the back of his icy hand, knocking her onto the floor. "Leave James alone, or I will kill you in such a horrendous way that your mother will take her own life when she finds your limp body."

Her mouth gaped open as Mr. Mason's spirit rippled and faded until he'd completely vanished. What on earth? It was still shocking to see Mr. Mason as a controlling, malevolent spirit instead of the quiet doctor who the whole island had admired.

Pulling herself up off the floor, she drew a deep breath to calm herself. *You and James are okay. That's all that really matters, and things will be better tomorrow.* She stood at her dresser, mindlessly brushing knots out of her hair, when a family photo caught her eye. Julia couldn't have been more than three, and her grandmother held her tight as if she were a prized possession.

Julia's grandmother's old stories about sending evil spirits to their final resting place twisted through Julia's mind. Perhaps it was time for a family reunion, and her mother didn't need to know. She climbed into bed. As she drifted off to sleep, the old stories wove their way into her dreams.

The story about her great-uncle John's wife, Vanessa, had always raised the hairs on Julia's arms. The couple had been married for only a month when John's ship had gone missing during a raging storm. Nana's grandmother had never liked Vanessa and had lied to her, saying John had met a certain death.

Devastated, Vanessa walked into the ocean wearing her wedding dress, with a ballast stone chained to her ankle. She carried the stone in her hand until the water was almost neck deep. When she let it go, a tall wave pulled her under, slamming her body against a rocky shelf. John's ship safely returned to the island a week after her death.

One night, Vanessa's spirit visited him. Realizing he couldn't see her, she turned her focus to tormenting Nana's grandmother, a well-known empath. Thanks to her abilities, she was able to bargain with Vanessa not to harm their family. But John never remarried; his grief over losing Vanessa due to his mother's betrayal was too great.

Julia had never seen it for herself, but some locals claimed to have seen a woman in white wading in the water, calling for her lover.

12

ELAINA

2021

Elaina's eyes burned as she opened them, and her wrists ached. Moving to soothe them, she realized her hands were bound. "Hey, why did you bring me here?" No one answered, but as Elaina's eyes adjusted, she took in the room. Someone had placed her on a firm bed with a faded but clean-looking comforter; chintz curtains covered the windows, and trophies topped with cheerleaders and majorette figurines covered warped wooden shelves. Elaina wasn't from a wealthy family. What could an aging nurse possibly want from her?

A door in another room slammed, and she jumped. Voices spoke in a hushed tone, making it difficult to make out the words. Elaina shifted to project her voice as much as possible. "Hello, can you hear me? Please tell me what is going on!" No one responded. She huffed and swallowed the tears that threatened to splash down her cheeks.

The chatter stopped, and footsteps approached the room where she was being held captive. Whispers were exchanged once again. *Who was talking, and what were they saying?* The doorknob turned, and so did Elaina's stomach. *Oh, God. Here we go.*

As the door inched open, her heart palpitated. Glenda stood in the doorway with a tray of food and a pitcher. "I know you have a lot of questions, and we'll get to them, eventually. For now, all you need to know is you're safe. Even if we were the dangerous type, which we're not, we need your help. Your babies need to be alive and well for us to get what we need. So eat up, get some rest. There's a TV in here, and I'll bring you a few books. Think of this as an all-expenses-paid vacation where you don't have to go sightseeing or worry about how you look in a bathing suit."

Heat rose from Elaina's chest to the top of her scalp. "What in the hell is going on? Nothing you said makes sense. You're dangerous enough to kidnap me. That's all I need to know. This is no dream vacation! You need to let me go!" Clenching her jaw, she fumed. How could she possibly help Glenda?

Glenda straightened the quilt at the bottom of the bed. "I'm afraid we can't just yet. You need to try to calm yourself. It's not good for the babies when you're in distress. I'll turn on the television for you. How does a home decorating show sound? Those always take my mind off whatever is going on in my life. Oh, and you need to eat to keep up your energy. Don't forget that you're eating for three now." She placed the food tray on a nearby table and poured her a glass of water. "Eat up. I'll be back to check on you later."

Elaina pulled herself upright. "No! You need to let me go! My family is definitely looking for me, especially my brother-in-law, who is a police officer. He will find me, and you will go to prison for a very long time. If you let me leave right now, I'll tell my family that I couldn't find them, so I took a ride share car instead. And the car broke down. It's still early enough that my story would be believable." She forced a weak smile, hoping to convince Glenda; maybe it would work, and she could go home to her family. That was the best-case scenario for everyone.

"That won't be happening. I forgot that we need to change how your hands are tied so you can eat. I'll be right back." Glenda walked out of the room, and the hushed whispering began once again. Who was Glenda's accomplice? Did they know what she'd done and why? That was still a mystery to Elaina. There wasn't a huge ransom to claim. She lived in an ordinary condo in an average city with her perfectly normal guy.

Glenda returned with a teenage girl, with wiry red ringlets, in tow. "This is my Lauren. She's going to help me make sure you don't try to escape." Glenda cut the zip ties that had bound Elaina's hands together and attached her left hand to the bed railing. "I'm sorry, but this is necessary."

"But why? Why do you want me here? I'm wracking my brain trying to figure out what I could possibly offer you." Elaina locked eyes with Glenda, who patted her free hand. *Ugh! Why is she touching me?*

"Sweetie, we'll get to that very soon. We're just waiting for my sister to join us. She can tell the story so much better than me. As long as you cooperate, you needn't worry. Now, eat up and get some rest. I'll be back soon. Lauren's going to keep you company."

Lauren peered out the window before turning to address Elaina's unrelenting stare. "My mom just wants what's best for me. Can you blame her? Don't you want that for your children?"

Elaina blinked. "What on earth do I have to do with your wellbeing? Help me understand." This made no sense. She'd never met this deranged family, so how was she responsible for their lives in any way?

"I'm sick, but you could help me get better," Lauren started.

"I don't understand. How could I help you?"

The door burst open, and Glenda, red-faced, grabbed a

handful of Lauren's fiery locks, pulling her out of the room. Elaina's jaw gaped as the girl shrieked.

"Let her go!" Elaina screamed, but Glenda didn't acknowledge her request. Clearly, the woman thought Lauren had revealed a secret, but Elaina still didn't understand. She didn't have medical training or a *magic* wand to wave over Lauren's body. How could she save anyone's life?

Oh, no—magic! Elaina gasped. Did this have something to do with her abilities? Glenda must have overheard her family's conversation at the hospital. Six years ago, Granny Mason had explained that she'd passed on her gifts to communicate with the dead to all three of the Nelson sisters. But becoming pregnant with twins had given Elaina the new gift of seeing the memories of dead people while using an object that belonged to them. How could these abilities prevent a sick person from dying?

Why did Granny have to cross over for good just when Elaina needed her the most? She'd helped Blake and Brittany during their struggles. Who would help Elaina? Of course, her family would do their best, but how would they track down Glenda's location if that was even her real name? Elaina pulled at the zip tie that bound her hand, but the plastic pulled at her skin, leaving red marks.

A car engine rumbled outside the house. Had the elusive sister arrived? Would Elaina finally discover the reason for her kidnapping? Her stomach growled; the food on the tray remained untouched. Could she trust that it was safe to eat? Did she have much of a choice? The babies needed food, and who knew how long she'd be stuck in this prison. Biting into the sandwich, she braced herself for the worst, but thankfully, it was just a grilled cheese. She let out a sigh of relief and continued eating until a shrill scream echoed into her room. Who was that, and what had happened to them? Elaina gulped. *I thought they wouldn't hurt anyone!*

Someone tapped on the door. That's odd. Why knock now?

She scrunched her face and invited them to come into the room. A familiar-looking blond woman in her fifties, wearing a colorful dress, entered the room. The unsettling twinkle in her eye especially bothered Elaina. Where did she know this person from? Was she a bank customer from Elaina's days of working in a branch? Did she work with Todd?

The woman laughed. "My name is Heather. I see that you're trying to place me, but don't waste your energy. We haven't met, but you know my sister, not Glenda, our other sister. My twin, to be exact. Y'all got acquainted real good last year. She told our cousin, who has spiritual abilities, all about your family. It was too good to be true that you lived in the same town as us. Glenda and I knew it would be just a matter of time before you came to the hospital."

Elaina shook her head. "I think you've mistaken me for someone else. It's like I told Glenda, if you let me go, I won't tell anyone about this. I'll make up a convincing story to tell my family."

Heather chuckled. "You're not going anywhere. We've got plans for you, and it's time to get started." She put her hands in her pockets and patted the inside, digging for something. "I must have left it on the kitchen table. I'll be right back."

What object held that much importance? Elaina shivered. It was beyond creepy that these women had stalked her for the better part of a year. Now, her unborn children were wrapped up in a potentially dangerous situation, too. What was Todd thinking right now? Was he searching the hospital for her?

Heather slipped back into the room, her hand firmly grasping its contents. Elaina held her breath as the aging woman approached her bed. *Here we go!*

"Hold out your hand." Heather reached out to Elaina. "Now, we'll get to see if our theory about your abilities is right."

Cringing, Elaina opened her palm and closed her eyes. *Please, God, get me through this.* When she opened her eyes, Heather revealed a fossilized oyster shell. *What the hell? Who carried around an oyster shell?* Elaina's blood ran cold. This wasn't just any old shell, and Glenda and her family weren't just random strangers. *Heather must be Serena's twin!* The resemblance was strong, but the years hadn't been kind to the sea witch's sister. Then again, it might not be fair to compare a woman in her mid-50s to her identical twin whose appearance hadn't changed since the 80s.

The previous year, Elaina's family had fought against the spirits of a woman named Serena and 200 of her deranged followers. This ghostly crew had died in a tragic hotel fire on Sweetgrass Island, just off the coast of Isle of Palms, South Carolina, during the mid-1980s. Locals had dubbed the spirits *the mermaids* because they had been trapped in the waters of the Intracoastal Waterway since dying. Seeing Serena was at the bottom of Elaina's wish list, but it didn't look like she'd have a choice.

Heather placed the shell in Elaina's hand. "Say hello to my sister."

Elaina sighed, knowing she only had seconds before the darkness and the coinciding nightmare came.

13

SERENA

2020

S erena stood on the roof of the Mason bed and breakfast, looking into the luscious garden. She would have loved this place in life, but now, she wanted to destroy it and the people who'd made a happy life here. Perky little Brittany Nelson made Serena want to gag. Her cutesy smile and bouncy dark curls were too perfect to be tolerated. She needed to suffer, to understand pain, something Serena had experienced often.

When Serena's parents died in a car accident, she and her sisters were placed in separate foster homes. But she hadn't let the trauma of her childhood define her. In the 1980s, Serena graduated at the top of her grad school class and secured a job as the general manager for a soon-to-be-built boutique resort on Sweetgrass Island, close to Isle of Palms and Charleston.

The day the developers broke ground, the hotel was fully booked for the first month, primarily by celebrities and other A-listers. Despite having bounced from one foster home to the next, she had found success and stability as an adult. So many of her foster siblings couldn't say the same. To further seal her happiness as a young adult, she'd hired a private investigator to find her twin, Heather, and their other sister, Glenda. After three months of searching, he found a lead that took him straight to them.

Reconnecting with her sisters was everything Serena had wanted–someone to fill the void left by their parents' death. For the next six months, the sisters spent nearly every waking moment together, sharing stories, photographs and their plans for the future. As they rebuilt their relationship, the hotel walls rose, staking its claim as the Lowcountry's most chic new resort.

A week before the grand opening, the owners, Deedee and Reggie Sutton, hosted a celebration for the staff. Heather had joined Serena for the first part of the event, but she fell ill after dinner. Before her sister left, Serena took her aside and explained she had hidden some money away, and she wanted Heather and Glenda to use it to buy a house in Charleston.

They made plans to meet up for brunch the following day to discuss the location of the money. Unfortunately, life doesn't follow the expected path. Deedee and Reggie fired fireworks from their boat at the end of the celebration, floating mere feet away from the hotel building on the Intracoastal Waterway.

Two sheets to the wind, Reggie accidentally shot a firework straight into the midsection of the hotel. The flames cut through the teak trimmed building like a knife through butter. Initially frozen in place, Serena shook herself back to reality, helping younger staff members and children to the stairwell furthest from the flames. But the fire had weakened the structure, sending them spiraling to a deadly landing.

After the fire, Serena came to, floating in the water. Colors had lost their brilliance, and the scenery that had once captivated her imagination repulsed her. Time didn't pass the same way in death, but if she had to guess, a month had vanished before she fully accepted her fate. As she allowed herself to embrace her new existence, she found others who had died in the fire. Over time, they became a family, developing an army that could take down anyone who threatened their peaceful existence in the waterway. The locals called them mermaids, a title they adopted.

One day, while standing on the bank, she saw a familiar face–Heather! Serena ran to greet her sister, waving frantically while screaming her name, but she didn't respond. Why couldn't her sister communicate with the dead? She buried her head in her hands, wishing for the earth to swallow her spirit whole. When she looked up again, Heather had disappeared. And just like that, Serena had lost her sister for the third time.

Serena sniffed, coming out of her trance. She'd give anything to talk to Heather or Glenda, but this wasn't the time to think about the past. Brittany and her sisters were up to something. They'd mastered pulling the wool over people's eyes, making them believe they were delicate, angelic creatures. *Ick. As if!* Serena saw them for what they really were–spoiled little bitches who always got their way. They were almost as irritating as Dee Dee and Reggie's kids, Parker and Maggie.

Apparently, one of Brittany's sisters had been involved with Parker when he was alive. *What a mistake!* Sure, he was a snack, but one with extra calories and no substance. No matter, she could easily capture these wannabe evil spirits with her special bottling spell. Best of all, Serena had tricked the Nelsons into bringing the Suttons together in one spot. She'd never been lucky enough to see the devilish twins together for more than a few moments; now, she could send them away permanently.

Serena's heart glowed as she thought of having revenge on Dee Dee and Reggie for burning down the hotel and killing hundreds of people. Not only that, but she could also trap the perky Nelson sisters, making them do her bidding. They could serve as a vessel to communicate with Heather and Glenda.

Serena could finally share where she'd hidden her savings. Money didn't do her any good in the afterlife; she'd always intended for her sister to use the money, anyway.

14

ELAINA

2021

Elaina woke eye to eye with Lauren. "Agh! Get away!" She shooed the child, who jumped back against the wall. "Haven't you ever heard of personal space?" *What a strange kid! As if being in Serena's body wasn't frustrating enough!* Elaina had hoped she would wake up in her bedroom to discover the kidnapping was another pregnancy-induced nightmare. No such luck. The throbbing in her wrist told her this was a legitimate emergency.

Lauren giggled. "Of course, silly. I just wanted to know if you found out where to get the money."

"What money?" Elaina blinked. She wouldn't give them the satisfaction of knowing the contents of her dreams yet. That would give them too much power. This way, she could leverage her knowledge, or lack thereof, as needed.

"Don't lie to me, just because I'm a kid. I know you dreamed about Aunt Serena. I heard you say her name in your sleep." Lauren folded her arms over her chest and pouted. "Mom! Elaina is awake! Come here!"

Footsteps thundered from across the house up to the bedroom door. When the knob turned, Elaina gulped. Lauren was right; it was easier to fib to her. Would Glenda and Heather see right through her story? All she could do was pray not to give away anything.

The older women entered the room, taking seats around the bed. Heather looked at Glenda, who nodded and started rattling off questions. "Did you see Serena? Where was she? Did she mention the money? Where is it? Don't leave out any details!"

Elaina yawned and stretched. "I don't have a clue what you're talking about. I didn't dream at all. Why don't y'all just try using a spirit board to contact her? If you won't let me out of here, I think I'll take another nap. Being pregnant has zapped my energy." She closed her eyes halfway and cuddled the faded quilt.

Heather jumped to her feet and got in Elaina's face. "Listen here, girlie–I don't play around. Glenda's the nice one in the family. Maybe she gave you the impression that you have a choice whether you're going to help us, but that ain't so." She pulled a knife out of her dress pocket and held the blade taut against Elaina's lower abdomen. "I don't want to hurt you or your babies, but I will if you don't tell us what we need to know." *How could Heather be so ruthless?* These little lives inside of Elaina's body couldn't protect themselves, and she couldn't do much with one hand chained to the damn bed! Helping these women was the last thing she wanted to do, but it was the only way to save all three of their lives.

Elaina huffed. "Fine. Whatever. I dreamed about Serena. It was the night she tried to kill my entire family. See why I'm not in a hurry to talk about her or to help you?" She wiped a tear away from her cheek.

Heather applied more pressure to the blade. "What about the money?" *Gulp! I guess I'll have to cave after all.* Elaina fought the urge to smack the knife away from her stomach. Infuriating a bully when you can't fight back never helps.

"She mentioned hiding some money, but she didn't say

where she'd hidden it. I woke up before she gave any details, and that's the truth."

The knife burned her skin, stretched out on either side of the blade. Glenda pulled it, along with Heather's hand, away from Elaina. "We don't want to use force to get information from you. Do you understand that? Can you please cooperate from now on?"

Elaina nodded, but Heather still locked eyes with her, burning holes right through Elaina as she and Glenda left the room. Lauren stayed behind, helping Elaina pour a glass of water and find something to watch on TV.

Afterward, Lauren hugged her. "I'm sorry if Aunt Heather scared you. She and mom are really worried I'm going to die. If we don't get the money, I probably will. I'm not so afraid, though. Life hasn't been easy for me. Sometimes, I wonder if death will be a huge relief. I'm pretty sure it will be. Don't worry about me; I'm not suicidal, just a realist." As Lauren hopped out of the room, sunlight highlighted the tips of her fiery ringlets.

Poor kid. Knowing you're going to die at that age had to be tough. She called out to Lauren, who returned to the room a moment later. "Did you need some more food, water or somethin'?"

"No. I wanted to ask what is wrong? Why do you think you're going to die? Are you sick?"

Lauren sighed. "When I was born, I had multiple birth defects. I've already had a kidney transplant and a bunch of other random operations. Now, I'm on the list for a liver transplant, but we don't have the money for the operation. My dad died last year, so we live on just mom's salary. She makes a good living, and if I were healthy, we'd have more than enough money. My doctor appointments, surgeries and medications have almost bankrupted us."

How horrific for this kid to live with that amount of guilt! Maybe Elaina should be more helpful. That's the least she could do for Lauren. If Elaina's babies were in trouble, she'd want people to help them. *Oh, God! What am I saying? My unborn children are in trouble! Please, God, help my family find us!*

As if she read Elaina's mind, Lauren patted her stomach. "When will your babies be born?"

Elaina sighed. "I'm not entirely sure because I haven't gotten a due date from a doctor yet." She leaned upright and grabbed Lauren's hand. "I'm terrified something is going to happen to my babies if I don't go home and get to my doctor this week. Do you understand?"

Lauren nodded but teared up a moment later. "But if you leave, you won't help us find the money, and I'll die. What will my mom do if I'm not here? She's already lost my dad and would only have Aunt Heather." Elaina's heart shattered into a million pieces. She didn't want anything to happen to the girl. Even if Elaina didn't care about Lauren, how could she expect a child to comprehend the repercussions of not getting timely prenatal care?

"Listen to me. I promise that I will tell you when I find out where the money is hidden. That money belongs to your family. I'd never try to keep it from you, especially since you need it. But I don't have to be here to help you. Please ask your mom and aunt to do the right thing and let me go. I won't turn you guys in to the police. I'll lie to my family. I don't want anything to happen to you."

Elaina held her breath, waiting for Lauren to respond. Could this plea for help work? It was doubtful, but asking was the only way to know for sure.

Lauren paced the room, looking over her shoulder as if she expected someone else to pop into the room. After a couple of minutes, she finally settled and moved closer to the bed. She leaned in close to whisper. "My mom has to go to work tomorrow morning. Aunt Heather takes sleeping pills, so she always sleeps late. I'll try to bust you out of here when my mom leaves. I'd better go for now. They'll be coming back in here to check on you." Wringing her hands, the girl ran toward the door. At the same time, the door swung open, nearly hitting Lauren in the face. She shrieked and stumbled backward.

Heather poked her head into the room. "What in heaven's name is going on in here? Lauren, why aren't you in bed yet?" Elaina sucked in a deep breath and closed her eyes. Had they been caught? Would Heather lock Lauren up in her room to keep her away from Elaina? How would she escape, then?

Lauren straightened herself and lowered her eyes. "You just scared me. I'm leaving now."

"Good girl. Be sure to kiss your mom goodnight. She's had a rough day. See you in the morning, love." Lauren cut her eyes at Elaina, took a deep breath and walked out the door. *Whew! Thank goodness–it seems like she bought it.*

After the door closed, Heather turned to Elaina. "So, now that you know what we're after, we need you to go back into Serena's memories and find the money."

Elaina bit her lip and shook her head. She didn't want anything to do with Serena. The spirit had held her family hostage and threatened their existence only a year ago.

Heather threw up her hands. "Do you understand what I'm saying?" She paced the floor, walking toward the door but pivoting to stare at Elaina sharply.

"I'll do my best," Elaina shrugged. "I never know what to expect when I dive into a memory. In some ways, it's like taking a trip to a place I've never been, and in others, it's like deja vu."

"I don't think you're getting the point. You will make it happen or else."

"Or else what?" Horrible thoughts swirled through Elaina's mind, but she forced herself to smile. She couldn't let Heather get the best of her. It was the only upper hand she had at the moment.

Heather lit a cigarette and puffed a cloud of smoke into Elaina's face. "I thought that my knife and I made it clear earlier–we'll have to dispose of you and your babies. It wouldn't bother me in the least. I know Lauren told you she's dying.

She's all my sister has, so if you don't help us save her, why should we care if you and your twins die?" Glaring at Elaina, Heather pulled a silver and mother of pearl engraved compact out of her pocket and dropped it into Elaina's hand.

The monogram, SJE, caught Elaina's eye before the familiar warmth and emptiness washed over her body, sending her to another place and time.

15

SERENA

1987

Looking over her shoulder, Serena slipped her compact into her interior jacket pocket before unzipping her hot pink and black alligator skin fanny pack. Patting the interior zippered pouch, she made sure the rolled bills were still in place. She let out a sigh of relief when the hefty stack sank lower into the purse. Where could she hide the money for safe-keeping? She didn't want questions from her regular bank teller, a friend from high school, who asked the most irritating personal questions about her deposits.

Why was she so nosy? It wasn't any of her business how Serena had come up with $80,000. She'd inherited the money from an older man she'd dated on and off throughout her 20s. The decade was coming to a close in exactly a week. The inheritance had surprised her, as the man had ex-wives and children who lived up and down the Eastern seaboard.

But this milestone birthday would be the beginning of Serena's new life. She'd just accepted a new job as the general manager of a prestigious new resort. Her years of busting her butt as a night-shift manager at chain hotels were finally over. The nest egg, along with a regular sizable income, would be enough to buy and maintain a comfortable home in Charleston and set her sisters up with their own house next door.

Although they'd just been reunited, the private detective had confirmed that their living arrangements were less than desirable. Serena was sure they would agree to move, and she needed them as much as they needed her. Reconnecting with them had healed so many wounds left by their family's tragic past. A new home would bring them together and provide safety and security as their sisterhood blossomed once again.

Although things were finally looking up for Serena, the cobblestones under her feet mirrored her emotional state, uneven and full of unexpected rough patches. She took soothing breaths and walked to White Point Gardens, alongside the Battery in downtown Charleston. The Cooper River sparkled a deep bluish-gray, with tufts of green, shimmering spartina grass poking through its entry.

The Lowcountry was undeniably the most beautiful place she could imagine living, even though the foster home that had brought her here had left an infinite number of emotional and physical scars. It was time to leave all of that behind her and move on to start a new beginning—one she and her sisters could create together.

Serena looked at her watch; she had exactly an hour until she needed to be at the Isle of Palms Marina to take a boat to Sweetgrass Island for her first team meeting at the resort. She'd hired some of the best hospitality professionals in the area, and the hotel owners had given her carte blanche to run the hotel side of the resort as she saw fit, but she couldn't be late. That wouldn't set the right tone with her team. All the same, she didn't want to continue carrying the large stack of bills in her fanny pack. Someone was bound to notice.

Looking over her shoulder to see if anyone was around, Serena approached the cannons that flanked the left-hand side of the garden. She observed the dark opening of one of the guns. No one would ever find her money in there! Serena looked around and found a long tree branch lying beneath the billowing oak trees.

She took off her fanny pack, removing her wallet and keys and placing them inside her pocket. Tying the straps of the fanny pack to the branch, she carefully slid it into the cannon, bag first. Praying she could retrieve the bag, she tested her theory. *It worked!* The bag was still attached! She breathed a sigh of relief. Her money was safe for the time being. *Now it's time to get to work.*

16

ELAINA
2021

Elaina rubbed her stomach as she planned what she'd tell Heather, who must have left the room during Elaina's nap. These precious lives growing in her womb depended on her, and Heather had made it clear she didn't value Elaina or her children's lives. Once Elaina gave away the location of the money, she wouldn't have any reason for Heather not to kill her. She had to escape. If Lauren didn't follow through on helping, there had to be another way. Hopefully, an opportunity would present itself soon; that way, she could leave Lauren out of it altogether.

So many other questions whirled through Elaina's mind. Did anyone think Glenda could be the culprit? Had she been questioned? Surely, the hospital had cameras that had captured the kidnapping. Why hadn't she been arrested, or at least investigated?

What was Elaina's family doing to find her? With Clint being the police chief on Isle of Palms, she knew he had connections with officers across the Southeast. Elaina was positive her family members were doing their best, but with none of them familiar with the area, finding her would prove even more difficult.

The door popped open unexpectedly, and Elaina gasped. Lauren, dripping with sweat, held a pair of scissors in her hand. "Okay, it's now or never. My aunt's out cold."

Elaina shot up straight in the bed. Lauren had come through for her! Why had she doubted the child? "Thank you so much. I know this is a hard decision. I promise to try to help you try to find the money." What she didn't say to Lauren is that she planned to report Glenda and Heather to the police—if she ever got out of the house, that is.

Lauren drew a deep breath, nodded and began cutting the zip ties, freeing Elaina's hands. This was it! She could go home and be with her family. She was going to be a wife and a mom, and that's all that mattered!

Elaina's legs buckled underneath her as she tried to stand. Weak from lying in bed, she pushed herself to straighten her body. As she regained her balance, she looked over at Lauren to see the color drain out of the child's face.

"Lauren, are you okay? Do you need to sit down?" Elaina gestured toward the bed.

"No, I'm okay." The girl looked up with a pained expression on her face before she crumpled into a heap on the tile floor. The thud of her body hitting the tiles pained Elaina. She checked Lauren's pulse and breathing. Thankfully, both seemed to be relatively normal. What concerned Elaina the most was the knot forming on the girl's head where she had hit the edge of the bed frame as she'd fallen.

How could she get help? Heather was an unfriendly beast of a woman. If she discovered Lauren had freed Elaina, there would be hell to pay for both of them. Elaina sighed and grabbed the scissors that had fallen from Lauren's hands. Hopefully, the raging wind and rain, punctuated by a clap of thunder, would help cover the noise.

What if Heather wasn't as heavy of a sleeper as Lauren

thought? Would she come running through the door to see what had made such a loud noise? What if she saw Elaina standing over Lauren with a pair of scissors in her hand? No question about it; Elaina had to run now. This was her only chance. Quickly, she slipped on her shoes and grabbed her grandmother's purse off the bedside table.

Elaina grasped the scissors firmly in her hand and began tiptoeing across the room. When she reached the door, she took a deep breath and gently pulled it open, unsure of what she'd find.

There was a stillness in the house. Heather must be out like a light. In the dimly lit hallway, she crept toward what she hoped was the living room, cautiously placing one foot in front of the other.

After a dozen calculated footsteps, she entered a light-filled room that took her breath away. Shelves covered with lush green plants seemed to take over the space, lending hope to the concept that life could thrive in this otherwise dismal home. There was something almost magical about their presence. It would be great if some of their vitality would spread to Lauren, giving her a chance to live a long, happy life. Elaina sighed. *Was it wrong to leave Lauren behind? No.* Wiping a tear from her eye, she cleared her throat. Elaina couldn't get help without leaving. Staying wouldn't help anyone.

She twisted her hands but charged ahead toward the front door. Clutching the worn brass doorknob, she twisted it clockwise. A heavy curtain of rain danced along the edge of the front porch, but it didn't matter. She had to go. Looking back over her shoulder, she leaned back into the living room, searching for an umbrella, a rain jacket or anything to provide protection.

A yellowing baseball cap hung on a hook next to the door. *It was better than nothing.* She pulled the hat onto her head and looked back into the room one more time. The room was still empty, but heavy footsteps boomed from Heather's room, leading to the room where Elaina had been held hostage.

Heather's muffled voice echoed as she called Lauren's name. The good news was Heather would help Lauren; the bad news was she knew Elaina had gotten loose. *Oh, God, please help me! Help my babies!*

Running into the rain, Elaina's shoes squished with every step. Where could she go? Houses lined each side of the road, but would someone help her? Elaina ran to the end of the street, not stopping until she reached a house without a garage or any cars in the driveway. The covered front porch gave her a place to catch her breath, but it wasn't the best place to hide long term. By now, Heather had certainly noticed that Elaina had run away. Being less than a two-minute drive from Heather wouldn't be good enough.

There had to be a more remote spot to take cover. A large gardening shed behind a house across the street caught her eye. That would have to do for the time being. At least no one would work in their yard or flower beds during a monsoon. *Thank God for small favors!*

Mud splashed onto Elaina's shoes as she sloshed her way to the shed. Teeth chattering, she steadied her hand to open the weathered door. Looking over her shoulder, she scanned the street for any sign of Heather. There wasn't a soul in sight. *Thank the Lord!* Ducking into the shed, she looked around for something heavy to barricade the door.

Dozens of small planters lined the walls. She zeroed in on a slightly larger ornate concrete pot—*perfect!* While Elaina squatted to lift the planter, her forearms strained under the weight. This wasn't a job for a pregnant woman, but there wasn't anyone else who could help. Elaina pushed the planter on its side, rolling it with her foot a couple of feet at a time.

Taking a deep breath, she muttered a prayer under her breath, "God, I know I've asked for a lot in my life, but help me get back home. These babies need their family, who already loves them more than anything." And her family needed her to fight for all three of their lives. She had to keep going; a little rain couldn't stand in the way of getting back to Todd and the rest of her family. With a renewed sense of purpose, Elaina pushed the pot the rest of the way to the door. Bending her knees, she secured the entry.

Elaina stood up again and looked around for somewhere to sit. A pair of lightly rusted beach chairs had been propped up the corner. She grabbed one and pried it open, despite its rusty state. The scraping sound took her back to playing on rusted swings at the beach on Isle of Palms as a kid. Granny Mason had always said that everything rusted at the beach.

The salt air degraded everything, eating away at its substance until it finally crumbled. For Elaina and her sisters, salt air was a sign that the ocean and their serenity were within reach. Not all people found the ocean's charms rejuvenating; maybe it was because the salt air had oxidized their souls. *Or perhaps I need to stop thinking of such weird things and rest.*

Sighing, she pulled an oversized beach towel off a nearby shelf and draped it over herself as she lowered her body into the low-slung chair. Her stomach rumbled, but eating would have to wait. Right now, she needed to get some shuteye. For the time being, she was safe and inside a relatively dry spot. Who knew how long the raging storm would last? Once it let up, someone might need to get into the shed, and that wasn't a thought she wanted to entertain.

Trying to clear her mind, Elaina tucked the frayed edges of the towel under her legs. When sleep didn't come easily, she opened her grandmother's purse, allowing herself to be swept away for another adventure in Granny Mason's young adult life.

17

JULIA CAROLINE

1960

Julia Caroline grinned as she took in the artwork in her grandmother's sitting room. The bold colors never sat well with Mama, but Julia always thought the Impressionists' paintings added flair to Nana's eclectic home.

After a few moments, Nana brought a tray with tea and something called granola bars that she'd made earlier that day. There was something delightful about the chewiness of the oats combined with raisins and cinnamon. Julia made a mental note to get the recipe to add to her collection.

As Nana poured the tea, Julia could tell her grandmother wanted to ask why she was visiting. Since Mama frowned upon Nana's ideas about ghosts, the afterlife and many other topics, Julia hadn't stopped by her grandmother's home without her whole family in tow in years. There wasn't an easy way to bring up the supernatural, especially when discussing a personal experience. So, Julia dove into the conversation head first, just like she did when taking her first swim in the frosty Atlantic every spring.

She looked at her hands. "Thanks for letting me barge in on you today without advance notice. I've had some bizarre things happen to me lately, and you're the only one who can help me. Before I say anything else, do you promise not to tell my parents, especially my mother? They wouldn't understand what I'm about to say."

Nana smiled. "Of course. I was wondering when we'd have this conversation about the spiritual world. I've been looking forward to it for quite some time."

Julia's jaw dropped. "How did you know that's what I wanted to talk about?"

"Child, I've suspected that I'd passed down my gift to communicate with the dead to you, just like my grandmother passed it down to me. Now, what's troubling you?"

Julia shared how Mr. Mason's angry spirit had stalked her and repeatedly threatened her life. The concern in her grandmother's eyes was apparent, but she sighed and sat silent for a moment.

"This sounds like a vengeful ghost, but you can certainly send him on to the Other Side. We have a full moon tomorrow, so we'll work our magic then. Do you have any friends who are believers who can join us here?"

"Nancy will help us, and maybe Paulene will, too. They've both seen weird, unexplainable things."

"That would make four of us, which will be perfect. All good things happen in twos. You girls should get here around 10:30 tomorrow evening. You need to write a letter to Mr. Mason explaining why he needs to move on to his final destination. Oh, and don't forget to bring enough candles for each of us, a hand mirror and an open mind."

Julia gulped, but nodded. Nana held her only ticket back to normalcy. There was no way to bring Mr. Mason back from the dead, but maybe they could at least help him rest in peace, allowing the living to find some sense of contentment and happiness.

She began walking the two blocks from her grandmother's home to Palm Court. As soon as she reached her street, she ran inside her family's home and called her friends, who weren't speaking to each other. They wouldn't divulge the reasons for their fight, but Julia hoped these odd circumstances would help them mend any broken pieces of their friendship.

The next afternoon, Julia waited for her mother to leave for the market. Once she heard the screen door in the kitchen clank behind her mother, she ran through the house to collect the items Nana had requested. When she'd found the candles and mirror, she pulled out a sheet of stationery and a fine-tipped pen to write the letter to Mr. Mason. Trying to calm her shaking hands, she drew a deep breath and thought about the result she was hoping for — a happy marriage, a successful career and a house full of children when the time was right. These thoughts helped her relax enough to pen the letter.

Dear Mr. Mason,

You were a wonderful man and a caring doctor. James and I never meant you any harm. We're both still in shock and saddened by your passing. We'd looked forward to many years of beach week-ends, picnics in the park and holidays with your family. You and your wife were great parents to James, and I know he loves both of you dearly. We hoped to give you grandchildren for you to adore, eventually, and of course, they would have admired you in return.

Our greatest wish is for you to find peace and move on to your final resting place. Don't worry about James. He will finish medical school and pick up your practice where you left off as soon as he is licensed. Most of all, you can know that I will love him as sure as the sun rises in the East. I will always take care of him and put his needs first. I also promise to help James take care of Mrs. Mason and your other children. There isn't anything left for you to worry about in this world. Please move on to your great reward. Paradise awaits. Rest in peace.

Yours truly,
Julia Caroline

Julia sighed as she folded the letter and placed it inside her purse. That was the most challenging letter she'd ever written, but she meant every word. Hopefully, Nana's plan would work, and Mr. Mason would cross over to the Other Side without so much as looking over his shoulder. She knew James wouldn't be able to move on with his life as long as his father's restless spirit roamed the earth.

The rattling screen door pulled Julia out of her thoughts. She ran to the kitchen, expecting to see her mother's arms loaded down with groceries, but no one was there. A chill crept up her spine and tingled throughout her body. Had Mr. Mason come to pay her another visit? Julia shivered. This haunting had to end tonight; whatever odd things she needed to do would be worth it.

She went to the downstairs powder room to splash some water on her face. When she looked up in the mirror, a note had been written in the condensation—*See you tonight.* Screaming, she ran out of the room, colliding with her mother, who threw her hands up in the air.

"Julia Caroline, why in Heaven's name are you screaming like a banshee?"

Julia groaned. She couldn't tell her mother the truth. "The hot water burnt my hands while I was washing them."

"Child, you scared me to death. I thought someone was trying to kill you."

Julia frowned and muttered under her breath, "That might not be too far from the truth."

"What did you say? Should I be concerned about you? Is someone trying to hurt you?"

"No, Mama. Don't worry about me. By the way, I'm going out with Nancy and Paulene this evening, and I'll probably stay the night with one of them."

Her mother's eyes widened. "If there's something you need to tell me. I'm always here to listen to you."

"Thanks, Mama. Everything's okay. I promise." Julia shifted her weight from foot to foot. She hated lying to her mother, but it couldn't be helped in this situation.

"Alright. I'm going to start dinner. Can you make sure your brothers and sisters are getting cleaned up? I want everyone presentable and at the table by 6:30."

"Yes, ma'am." Julia walked upstairs and collected her younger siblings from the den. "Y'all need to get ready for dinner before Daddy gets home." They groaned in unison but pulled themselves away from their books and toys. Her youngest sister, Sally, stuck out her tongue in passing. This is exactly why Julia needed to get away from her parents' home. She basically served as a third parent to these ungrateful little heathens. With everything going on with Mr. Mason, she didn't have time to worry about their sassy attitudes.

When their father arrived home from work, the family gathered around the table, and Julia gave the blessing for the food. She was grateful for her parents and everything they had done to provide for the family. It just wasn't the type of life she was rushing to have for herself. She and James would have several years of marriage under their belts before the babies came along.

After dinner, Julia excused herself and threw the items Nana had requested into an overnight bag before she said goodbye to her parents.

Her mother hugged her. "Call me if you need me anytime. I'm still worried about you. One day, you'll understand. I love you, child."

"Love you, too, Mama." She kissed her mother on the cheek and left to meet Nancy and Paulene outside of Nana's house.

As she approached the house, she saw her friends sitting on opposite sides of the porch, not looking at each other. They had to get over whatever had come between them. Julia knew it wasn't a boy who had caused the rift, as both of her friends were engaged to men who they'd been seeing since their adolescence, just like Julia and James. What else could come between friends who had loved each other as sisters since they'd started primary school?

Julia put her hands on her hips. "You two need to work out whatever is bothering you."

Paulene shrugged. "She's the one who has a bee in her bonnet. Not me."

Nancy glared at her and shook her head. "She knows what she did." *Ouch!* Nancy was feisty, but Julia had never seen her hold a grudge like this. What could Paulene have done that would irk their friend to this degree?

"I really don't. Please tell me so I can apologize for whatever I did, and we can move on with our lives."

"There isn't an apology great enough for telling Mr. and Mrs. Mason that James and Julia ran off to elope. Now, Mr. Mason is dead, and we're all having to deal with the repercussions from that. Not only did James lose his dad, but now, Julia Caroline is facing a horrific haunting all thanks to your loudmouth."

Julia gasped. "What are you talking about?" She turned to Paulene. "But how did you even know that we were planning to elope? I didn't even know until that night."

Nancy shot Paulene a dirty look. "She was having a late dinner with James' cousin and his wife when James stopped by to ask about the inn where they stayed on their wedding night. Paulene called me right after James left their house. She was having a fit, worried about you finishing high school and messing up your plans for college. She mentioned we should try to stop y'all from getting hitched before graduation. I thought I'd talked her off of the ledge, but I guess she couldn't keep her trap shut."

Paulene shook her head. "I promise I didn't tell a soul. I don't know how Mr. and Mrs. Mason found out."

Nancy rolled her eyes and looked over at Julia. "You can see why I'm not buying it. She obviously told her mama, who is best friends with Mrs. Mason. It doesn't take a rocket scientist to figure it out."

Julia didn't know what to believe, but nothing could be done to change what had already happened. "Look, y'all. No one wanted Mr. Mason to die. Even if Paulene tried to stop us from eloping, it doesn't mean she's responsible for this whole mess. Let's just get through tonight and worry about the rest later. Okay?"

Both of her friends nodded, but something told her their friendship would never be the same. Julia would just have to work extra hard to bring them back together.

Before anyone could say another word, Nana came out to the porch and stared at Julia and her friends. "Young ladies, what is all this racket? Are you trying to raise the dead? I'm pretty sure those resting in Bonaventure Cemetery in Savannah heard you. And I thought we were trying to send the spirits away tonight, not wake them."

"Sorry, Nana." Julia gave her friends a pointed look, daring them to say another word. "We're done fussing at each other. Aren't we?" Paulene and Nancy nodded.

Nana drew a deep breath. "Good, because we're gonna need to work together, not against each other tonight. Did you bring everything I asked for?"

Julia grabbed the contents of her overnight bag to show her grandmother, who gave an approving thumbs up.

The moonlight reflected in Nana's eyes, giving them an enchanting glow. "It's almost midnight. We need to plant your letter to Mr. Mason as close as possible to the last place you saw him, which was at your house, right?"

"Yeah, but we don't have to plant it there, do we? You know how my mother feels about anything supernatural."

"No, we'll go right to the edge of my property line. That should be good enough," Nana said. *Whew! Thank goodness!*

The four women walked to the fence that separated Nana's yard from her neighbor's and dug down a foot into the earth before placing the letter in the hole, along with some seeds. Nana explained the seeds would grow toward the light, helping carry Mr. Mason to his Heavenly home.

Julia Caroline looked to her grandmother for further direction, but the matriarch had already begun handing candles to the other women and lighting them, using an antique cigarette lighter. When Nana gave Julia her candle, she instructed her to pray, sincerely asking for Mr. Mason's soul to be transported to its final resting place.

She wiped her sweaty palms on her skirt and started her prayer, "Please bless our home and our family and allow Mr. Mason to cross over to his final destination. We want to cleanse our lives of any evil spirits that are in our presence. Amen."

Nana pulled the women into a circle and asked them to repeat Julia's prayer with her three times. The stillness in the air was unsettling. Julia expected Mr. Mason to appear at any moment. After an uneventful minute or two, Nana instructed her to hold the hand mirror up to her face and look just past her reflection.

What happened next took her breath away. Mr. Mason's face showed up in the mirror as if he were standing directly behind her. Julia was momentarily paralyzed with fear. When she was able to move, she exhaled loudly.

Nana winced. "I'm guessing he showed up in the mirror."

Julia whispered her confirmation and closed her eyes, hoping to block out what she'd just seen. If she never saw Mr. Mason's evil sneer again, it would be too soon.

"Hallelujah! That means it worked!" Nana clapped and did

a little dance. If everything was right in the world again, why did Julia feel so nauseous?

"Does that mean he's gone for good, now?" Julia asked. *Please say, "Yes!"* She and James needed it to be so. They were ready to start their lives together, and if Mr. Mason's spirit was truly gone, there was one less obstacle standing in their way.

"It should, but there is a more definitive way to seal the deal. If you could get your beau to marry you tomorrow, that would make it a sure thing. The act of a life event like a wedding or birth makes all the difference in the finality of death. It shows the dead what they can no longer do, convincing them to move along."

Julia nodded, motioning for everyone to come in for a hug. "I couldn't have done this without all of you! Thank you so much for supporting me through this bizarre, frightening time in my life! I guess I'd better go find my groom, so we can make this thing stick!" Julia waved at her grandmother and friends before running to the Mason household with a vengeance.

As she knocked on the door, she planned to tell Mrs. Mason the whole story and that she and James were getting married tomorrow, regardless of her opinion on the matter.

Luckily, James answered the door, wearing his robe and pajama pants. She lunged at him. "We have to get married tomorrow. No ifs, ands or buts about it!"

He grinned. "What's all this about?"

She kissed him furiously and pushed him up against the front door, pressing her body against his.

"Never mind. You're the boss." He kissed her back. "I'll pick you up in the morning."

As she said goodbye to him, she knew nothing would stand in their way this time.

PART II

ELAINA 2021

18

The rumbling of a car engine, followed by the obnoxious beeping of a car remote, woke Elaina. She jumped to her feet, listening for the driver's next move. Hopefully, whoever had pulled into the driveway wasn't in the mood to landscape their yard. Just in case, she looked around for a place to hide. Gardening equipment and beach gear filled almost every corner of the small shed.

She darted to the corner where she'd retrieved the beach chair. Crouching, she pulled the chair and towel over herself and formed her body into a tight ball. The position was uncomfortable, but she had to attempt to blend into the pile of beach umbrellas and shovels.

Someone walking in the gravel driveway caught her attention. Suddenly, the doorknob turned, and Elaina prayed silently, *Oh, God, help me! I should never have fallen asleep.* A shrill creak escaped when the door opened, followed by a thud as it hit the planter.

A deep grunt came from the other side of the door, and Elaina could hear someone muttering as they continued to struggle to open the door. When the planter toppled over out of the way, Elaina hugged her stomach. *My babies don't deserve to be in this situation.*

What would they do if they found her? Call the police? She bit her lip. That would be perfect. Then, she could spill the whole story to the authorities. But then again, they might not be so kind. What if the homeowner shot her on sight? After all, Elaina had broken into their potting shed. For all they knew, she was there to rob or murder them. She shivered and fought the urge to throw up.

Elaina squeezed her eyes shut, unable to bear watching as someone discovered her hiding spot. Her muscles tensed as metal clanking against metal echoed through the small space. Were they almost done? The door creaked again. *Oh, great–they have company!*

"C'mon, Daddy. I want to go to the indoor pool at the community center," a little voice squeaked, followed by stomping on the plywood floor. "Hurry, hurry. I wanna go now."

"Hi, hang on, kiddo. Go see Mama for a few minutes. I need to grab the beach towels and make sure the roads aren't blocked. Several of the roads washed out during the storm. I had to turn around instead of going to Grandma's house this morning."

"Okay, but hurry, Daddy!" The door slammed shut, and Elaina's heart pounded. At least there was only one person to hide from now. Unfortunately, it was the one who could do more harm. Why couldn't the little one have stayed instead?

The umbrella in her hiding spot shifted, and she held her breath. *Please grab any other beach towel; leave the one on top of me alone!* A cool burst of air sent the hairs on her neck on end. She tilted her head upward, and a muscular man held the towel that once covered her. She stared back at him, frozen in place, with his jaw gaping. *Shit! I'm in too deep now to let the police find me here. Would they even believe me?*

She pushed the remnants of her crumbling haven aside and

ran past the man, knocking over a stack of beach chairs on her way outside. Trapped behind the pile of rusty chairs, the man snapped into action, reaching out to grab her. Elaina pushed over several of the planters in hopes of further trapping him before she ran outside. *What in the hell am I doing?*

"Hey! Wait! Come back!" The man called out to her, but she kept running, zigzagging through yards, in the opposite direction from Glenda's house. It wasn't possible to put too much space between her and her captors. Poor, sweet Lauren still needed her help, but she couldn't take a chance that the man in the shed would call the authorities or try to hurt her. She had no choice but to run and not stop until she was sure she could hide safely or get help.

Clouds filled the darkening sky, threatening to ruin Elaina's plan. Was there anywhere she could take shelter if necessary? Taking in her surroundings, she recognized some houses. *Why were they familiar?* She realized she was only about a mile from downtown. If she was lucky, she might run into a friend or at least a stranger with a friendly face. Then again, the rainy weather had likely scared away people who enjoyed the downtown restaurant and bar patio scene. Who wanted to park and walk in the rain only to sit in the tiny, cramped interiors of these businesses, whose outdoor spaces were the main attraction?

Just as rain droplets began pelting Elaina's head, the familiar eclectic architecture—a mix of skyscrapers and colonial buildings—came into view. The deserted streets confirmed her theory that the weather had scared off the typically boisterous crowd. Taking a soothing breath, Elaina realized she was only five blocks from the bank where she worked. With it being a Saturday, no one would be there, but that was fine. If she could get through the security checkpoints, she'd be able to call Todd from her office.

Finally, she glimpsed her reflection in the towering mirrored building. *I made it! Thank God!* She stepped up to the first security checkpoint and placed her thumb on the sensor. Nothing happened. *What? Why? Did they remove me from the approval queue? Did they give up on me already?* Maybe they thought she'd run away. Did that mean she didn't have a job?

Pressing her face up against the glass, she squinted, hoping to see a coworker. But the rain mixed with the cool December air had fogged the almost opaque tiles, making it impossible to see through them. As she pulled away from the glass, she became aware someone was staring at her. Gulping, she slowly turned around to see the man from the shed. How had he found her? She'd taken the least direct path possible, zigzagging through the streets between his house and downtown.

He threw his hands in the air. "Hey, there you are! Why in the hell were you hiding in my shed?"

Elaina stared at him and started to answer, but he cut her off. "You know what, it doesn't matter. I don't care what you were doing. I'll let the police worry about that." She turned away, frantically trying to get through the security checkpoint again.

"Are you trying to break into the bank now so that you can rob it? Yeah, I'm calling 9-1-1 right now."

Elaina refused to turn around again instead of focusing on steadying her trembling thumb long enough to scan it. She held her breath and murmured a prayer for help. As if to answer her prayers, the door popped open, followed by a buzz. She ran inside and slammed the self-locking door behind her.

Before running to her office, she turned around once again. The man had his cell phone up to his ear, undoubtedly calling the police. She'd just have to get to her office to place her own call to the police before any officers showed up.

The security guard had left his post near the elevators, so she pressed the up button with gusto. *Hurry, please!* Once inside the car, she chose the ninth floor, where her office was located. It was a race against time before the police made it there, but she had to try to call Todd. She needed him to know what was happening. The authorities weren't likely to buy her story in the least. Even if they would, how could she possibly summarize everything that had happened? Tears stung her eyes; crying was a time suck that she couldn't afford, even if it might give her some relief.

Fighting back the tears, she watched the red glowing floor-level numbers ascend on the digital display. The doors flew open on the sixth floor. Elaina scooted back into the corner and stared at the floor. Biting her lip, she waited for someone to join her. Her heart in her throat, she looked up slowly as the doors slammed shut. No one was there. *Whew! False alarm! Just three more floors to go!*

When the doors opened again, Elaina jumped. Looking at the display, a red nine blinked. She'd finally made it to her floor! The familiar rows of gray cubicles and sparkling glass encapsulated meeting rooms welcomed her. Nothing had changed except for the addition of a Christmas tree decked out in burgundy and gold decorations and a swag of garland strung across the receptionist's desk. She'd forgotten that the holidays were approaching. Maybe now she'd actually get to celebrate them with her family.

A warm rush flowed through Elaina's veins. This was the home stretch! She began running towards the management office wing, stopping only to punch in her security code at the entry point. Feet throbbing, she pushed through the pain and kept moving. At the end of the hallway, she came to the executive suite, where her office adjoined those that belonged to her boss and peers. Only one more security checkpoint stood in her way. She held her breath as she fumbled with the keypad. The door buzzed as it opened, and she cried tears of relief.

Bleary-eyed, she opened the door to her office and sat down at the desk. Elaina had never been so happy to be at work. Dialing Todd's cell phone number didn't feel natural. She was unsure of what to say to him, or at least where to start. He had to be wondering where in the hell she'd been for the past couple of weeks. As the phone rang, she cringed, but Todd's panicked voice made her forget her insecurities. "Elaina? Is that you? Please tell me you're okay!" His voice cracked, and he choked as if he were trying not to cry.

She sobbed while trying to explain her kidnapping and harrowing escape. Shaking, she couldn't calm herself. All she wanted was to disappear into Todd's tender embrace and hide there until their sweet twins were born. Then, they could build their family together.

"Elaina! I barely understood anything you just said other than that the police are coming to your office. Whatever you do, stay there. I'm coming to help you, and Clint is coming with me. He'll know what to say to the police. Don't try to talk to them until we get there. Get yourself some water and try to relax. We'll be there in five minutes; I promise! But don't hang up; Clint has a few questions for you."

"Okay. I love you. Hurry!" She wiped a tear from her cheek and answered Clint's rapidly fired questions about where she'd been. Her heart rate sped up, and breathing became a challenge.

"Hey, it will be okay! You're safe now. Breathe for me, Elaina. We're on our way, and we won't let anything happen to you. Remember, you have a lot of people on your side. I'm going to call my buddy from the sheriff's office and see if he can come over and help us. I'll call you back as soon as I talk to him."

She thanked Clint and hung up her phone. Bending down, she grabbed a bottle of water from the mini-refrigerator under her desk and collected a handful of peanut butter and chocolate candies from the basket on her printer stand. Thank goodness the office admin had restocked her stash. The sugar gave her exactly the boost that she needed to keep going.

Walking over to the sofa in her office, she dropped onto the cushions, drew two deep breaths and gulped down the bottle of water. No one other than her coworkers could get into the bank, not even the police. That was one good thing about working in a secure building. Todd and Clint would make sure everything worked out with the authorities. She vowed to close her eyes for just a few moments, but her body gave way, shutting down due to the stressful events she'd experienced. Drifting off to a dreamless sleep, she forgot about the world.

19

T he ringing of Elaina's phone woke her. *Oh, Lord! How long was I asleep?* She jumped to her feet and checked the Caller ID to see Clint's phone number. *Hopefully, they're outside, and this crap can finally end!*

Picking up the phone, she cleared her throat to shake off the sleepiness. "Hey! Are you guys here?" She stood a little taller and puffed out her chest in anticipation. "Are the police out there?"

Clint sighed and cleared his throat. "I wish we were there, and I doubt the police are there either. The roads are flooded out pretty badly. I tried calling my buddy at the sheriff's office and got an automated message, saying emergency crews are only responding to incidents involving a critical injury. The entire department is overwhelmed trying to help people who thought their cars could drive underwater. It's a disaster out there."

Elaina's chest deflated. "You're kidding. It's not that bad out here, just a little soggy. Maybe the downtown police are around. I could go try to find someone to help."

Clint cut her off, "Listen, that's not how these situations

work. Todd said that downtown has a better storm drainage system in place than the rest of the city; that must be why you could get around on foot. Everyone from the safer precincts would have been called to help in the flooded sections of the city."

"Bear with me a second." Elaina pushed the speakerphone button on her handset and walked over to the window. Clint was right. There wasn't a sign of a patrol car or even the man who had been angry with her for breaking into his shed. "Yep. No one is out there."

"Good. Now, listen to me. Stay put in your office, and lock your door. Todd and I will get you as soon as this water recedes a little. I'll call you when we're on our way."

Wiping away a tear, Elaina sighed. "Thanks, Clint. Tell Todd and my family that I love them." She was lucky to have a brother-in-law in law enforcement. He'd watched out for her family in so many ways over the years.

After hanging up the phone, Elaina tugged at her shirt, which was plastered onto her skin. She needed a shower and a fresh change of clothes. Thank goodness she kept a gym bag inside her office closet. Opening the closet door, she grabbed the tote bag and headed to the company's workout facility and locker room in the basement.

Stepping into the spa-like shower, she scrubbed away the sweat and dirt. The warm water massaged and cleansed her skin, helping her relax somewhat. Too bad she couldn't wash away what had taken place at Glenda and Heather's house. What a horrible experience, except for meeting Lauren. Her stomach lurched. *Oh, God!* She'd forgotten about Lauren. *Poor kid!*

Heather had been harsh to Elaina, but she'd made it clear that Lauren's wellbeing was her priority. She would make sure Lauren was okay, wouldn't she? Of course she would. But what if Lauren had severe injuries and an ambulance couldn't make it there due to the flooding? The room spun in circles, and

Elaina wretched. As much as she wanted to deny her gut instinct, she knew that she had to go back to check on Lauren.

Elaina quickly put on her workout clothes and pulled her wet hair back into a loose bun. Looking in the fogged mirror, she tucked a loose piece of hair into a clip and psyched herself up to return to the horrors she had escaped only hours ago. Would Heather lock her up again? It didn't matter–an innocent child was in danger. She had to try to help Lauren, regardless of the consequences.

She threw a couple of water bottles and some protein bars into the tote bag and decided she needed to fire off an email to Clint and Todd explaining why she had to go back. Biting her lip, she asked them to give her a little time before they tried to rescue her. Police busting into Glenda's house and arresting her and Heather wouldn't help Lauren get better.

The child needed normalcy. Even though Lauren's guardians had kidnapped Elaina, they had only done it to protect her. Sure, it was a misguided decision and illegal, but Elaina could almost understand their reasoning. She rubbed her stomach and said a silent prayer for the safety of her unborn babies.

Stepping off the elevator, she began running toward the last place she'd imagined she would ever go. Spanish moss-covered tree branches flapped in the wind, pointing toward her destination. *Am I really doing this? Yes–it's the right thing to do!* Elaina bit her lip and brushed her bangs out of her eyes. It was time to push aside her desire to turn around, run back to her office and wait for her knight in a shining SUV to rescue her.

As Elaina's feet hit the pavement, she considered the possible outcomes of returning to Glenda's house. In the best-case scenario, Lauren would be outside alone and doing well, and Elaina could take the girl back to her office until the police came. Elaina couldn't entertain the thoughts of the worst possible outcomes. Lauren was sweet, thoughtful and had helped Elaina escape, even though her well-being was at risk. This kid was a saint.

The dozen or so blocks between Elaina's office and the crumbling bungalow were a blur. Unfortunately, no one was outside, so there was no chance of a quick getaway. She stared at the chipped blue paint on the front door, drew a deep breath and knocked. *Oh, boy, this should be fun.* Looking down at her water-logged shoes, she anticipated the worst.

After a few moments had passed, Elaina looked over her shoulder and tried knocking again. "Hello, Lauren? Glenda? Heather? Anybody home?" The hairs on her neck stood on end as she became aware someone was watching her.

She turned around to see a middle-aged woman with blonde hair standing behind her. "Hey, I live next door. They took the girl to the hospital by ambulance." The woman adjusted her glasses and sighed.

Elaina swallowed. "When? Did she look okay?" *I'll never forgive myself if I'm too late.* She exhaled deeply.

Shaking her head, the woman frowned. "She was out cold when the EMTs came this morning, around 7:30. I've been praying for that kid ever since she got sick. It's a real shame."

Elaina frowned but thanked the woman and began running back toward downtown. The hospital was just a couple of blocks away from her office. She could make it there in 35 minutes or less. Hopefully, Lauren was holding up okay.

Approaching the downtown area, a familiar white Jeep Wrangler passed her, but she paid little attention until the driver pulled over to the shoulder and slammed onto their brakes. As the window rolled down, Elaina held her breath. *Ugh.* She didn't need any drama right now.

"There you are! Oh, my God! I'm so relieved." Elaina couldn't see the driver's face, but she didn't need to. Her heart expanded as she realized Todd was driving Clint's Jeep. How she'd missed him! They hadn't been able to celebrate her pregnancy like most couples. That precious moment of anticipation had been stolen from them. Momentarily paralyzed, thoughts rapidly fired through her mind; how could she explain what she needed to do? Would he understand and agree to take her to see Lauren?

What would happen to the kid if Elaina didn't make it to the hospital in time to tell Glenda where Serena had hidden the money all those years ago? Was the money still inside a cannon in Charleston? Even if the money was still there, could Elaina prevent Todd from pressing charges against Glenda and Heather?

Would the child be taken away from the only family she had? Who would take care of her? Would she survive such a change? *Stop being so negative! The kid is a fighter.* Lauren had survived the unfathomable already. Given the opportunity to receive the necessary medical care, she had a strong chance of beating her illness.

Todd opened the driver's side door and jumped out of the Jeep. "Hey, are you okay? Do you need me to help you get into the car?" He offered her his hand, but she shook her head, falling onto her knees, crying. Through her tears, she pleaded with him, "I need you to trust me. This won't make sense at all." She started explaining why she wanted to help Lauren and how Glenda and Heather weren't bad people; they just wanted Lauren to have a chance of surviving.

"What in the hell are you saying, Elaina? Are you crazy? There's no way I'm taking you back to those horrible people. Clint is back at our place, plotting a rescue attempt. Based on your description, we had a rough idea of where Glenda's house is, but he'll be amped to know exactly where they are. You know that I feel sorry for the kid, but we'll make sure she stays safe. I'm sure that is at the top of Clint's mind, too."

"You're not listening to me. Glenda and Heather just want to figure out where Serena hid her money so that they can go get it and save Lauren. I know where the money is, and I can help them. The kid has been sick for a long time. This is a life or death situation for her. I know that you'd do the same thing for our babies." Elaina patted her stomach and locked eyes with him. Couldn't he understand this desire to help a child?

Todd matched her gaze and shook his head. "They have brainwashed you somehow. You can't actually think they're doing the right thing. I know you wouldn't ever kidnap someone, and you know I wouldn't either. That doesn't make me any less of a father. It makes me practical, sane and someone who follows the law. If anything, that should make me a better parent."

There was no changing Todd's mind once he'd decided something. Elaina would have to figure out how to do this without him. Feeling conflicted was an understatement. She loved him deeply, and more than anything, she wanted to go home and curl up in bed. But her duty to Lauren was more important than her own desires. She couldn't let that kid down. So, she had to do something. As she struggled with finding a solution, a sharp pain gnawed at her abdomen. Grabbing her stomach, she screamed, "Something's wrong! I'm having stabbing pains."

Todd leaned over and gently placed his hand on her shoulder. "Show me where the pain is." She was lucky beyond belief to have such a loving guy.

She lifted her shirt and clutched the left side of her abdomen before letting out a cry. "It's so horrible. I can't stand this pain!" Biting the inside of her cheek, she looked up at him and winced.

Without saying a word, he scooped up Elaina and put her into the Jeep, helping her recline the passenger seat. He gently brushed a piece of hair out of her face and put on her seatbelt. "Don't argue with me about this; I'm taking you to the emergency room to get checked out. You've been through hell, and I want to make sure that you and the babies are okay. At least we're not too far away."

As Todd drove, Elaina's stomach throbbed. Elaina was

concerned about the twins. Seeing a doctor would help put her mind at ease, but a trip to the hospital would also allow her to check on Lauren.

Now, she needed a brilliant strategy for what to do once they arrived at the hospital. The car went over a pothole, and Todd muttered under his breath. She glanced over at him, gripping the steering wheel with white knuckles, and her heart swelled. He was obviously trying to get her there in a rush.

20

The unnerving wail of the ambulances flying into the hospital parking lot momentarily distracted Elaina. Thankfully, she got a reprieve from the sirens as Todd parked the Jeep under the portico. He handed the keys to the valet and helped Elaina get out of the vehicle.

"Do you think you can walk? Should I get a wheelchair?" Todd raised his eyebrows, but his gaze quickly softened.

Elaina nodded, applying pressure to her stomach to ease the pain. "I think I'll make it."

Walking inside to the waiting area, she told Todd to take a seat so she could sign in at the front desk. But he grimaced. "Um, I won't let you go anywhere by yourself like this." *Damn it!* Of course, he was too chivalrous to abandon her, even for a few minutes. How would she check on Lauren with him in tow?

After taking a deep breath, she put out her hand. "Look, babe, I'm feeling a lot better. It was probably just gas or something equally embarrassing. Welcome to being engaged to a pregnant woman. But you're right. I've been through a lot over the past couple of weeks. So have you. That's why you need to find the comfiest chair possible, put in your earbuds and stream some funny videos."

His nostrils flared, but he kissed her on the forehead and sat down in an oversized chair near a window. Elaina breathed a sigh of relief, turned around and approached the admissions desk.

"Hi, two things—I'm pregnant and having sharp abdominal pains. I just want to be checked out super quick; my friend's daughter was brought in earlier. My friend is waiting for me to get here to sit with the kid while she takes a break. Can you tell me if she's been admitted?"

A woman with graying hair looked up over her half-moon reading glasses. "What's her name and yours?"

Elaina provided the details and bit her lip as the nurse slid the glass partition across the reception window and picked up her phone. Who was she calling? What if the nurse wouldn't let Elaina go back to see Lauren? Maybe she could at least write a note for Glenda since she worked at the hospital. There had to be a way to help, and the timing was key.

Across the room, Todd's eyes were closed, his head drooping, and a little dribble of drool had pooled on his chin. *That poor sweet guy. Should I wake him? No. He needs to rest, and it will buy me some time. Assuming I get to see Lauren.*

Suddenly, the window slid open again, and the nurse motioned for Elaina to step closer. She moved toward the window, anticipating bad news. Fidgeting with her hands, she tried to calm herself as the nurse pursed her lips together.

"Lauren isn't doing so well, but Glenda confirmed you were as good as family, so you can go back to see her. Poor child; I've been watching her come in and out of this emergency room her whole life. It's heartbreaking. Just so you know, we love Glenda here."

Elaina nodded, drew a deep breath. "Thank you so much. Where do I need to go?"

"I'll buzz you in and take you to her room. You can let any of the nurses on her floor know when you're ready to get yourself checked out, and they'll help you get to where you need to be." When the door popped open, Elaina walked through and followed the nurse to a bank of elevators. They rode up four floors in silence and weaved through a maze of hallways and wings before the nurse finally stopped and knocked on a room door.

"Here you are. I'm praying for y'all. Something's gotta give for this girl." The nurse patted her on the shoulder and walked away.

Elaina groaned. She wasn't looking forward to seeing Heather and Glenda again, but at least she was stronger and more capable of defending herself this time around. She pushed the door handle and found herself face to face with Heather. *Great! This is going to be delightful!*

"Look, Glenda! Our long-lost friend is here. How sweet!" Heather pulled Elaina into the room by her arm.

"Oww! Let me go right now. I came to help y'all not to hurt anyone. I have some news I need to share with you."

"Unless you're telling us we're winning the lottery, I don't know what you could tell us that would help. Your supposed gifts, dreams or whatever you want to call them aren't that special. They didn't help us find Serena's money, so we can't afford to have Lauren airlifted to the specialist at the hospital in Nashville. Now, it's going to be too late, anyway."

Elaina looked past the sisters for the first time to see Lauren hooked up to a ventilator. Her skin was ashen, so white it was almost blue. A knot formed in Elaina's throat, and she fought the urge to cry. *Lauren couldn't die in this drab hospital room at such a young age.*

"You don't know that. And I know where Serena left the money. I can't guarantee it's still there, but I can go look for it."

While rubbing Lauren's arm, Glenda lifted her head and stared at Elaina. "I don't know why you'd help us after what we put you through, but if you find it in your heart, it will make all the difference." The mother looked like an empty shell of the woman Elaina had met almost three weeks before. Lauren's dire situation had to be wearing her down. As a nurse, she knew the odds were stacked against her child. That had to be the most frightening experience a parent could have.

Elaina frowned. "What you don't know about me is I would have helped your family if you'd just asked upfront. You didn't need to kidnap me to convince me to help you. Of course, I'll still try to do whatever I can. That's just how I was raised, but it's more than just that for me. I love Lauren as much as if she were my actual niece. She's the entire reason I came back."

Glenda sniffed as tears spilled out of her red, puffy eyes. "Bless you for loving my baby enough to help us in such a selfless way." She motioned to Heather to get up and whispered, "C'mon, let's give her a minute alone with Lauren. We can at least do that for her." Heather scowled but followed her sister out of the room without saying a word. And Elaina let out a sigh of relief.

When the door closed, she grabbed Lauren's frail hand. "I'm going to do everything I can to get the money so that you can get the treatment you need. Whatever you do, you can't give up. Keep fighting, kid. You're my superhero; you saved my babies and me. I want to be at your Sweet 16 party in a couple of years and watch you graduate from high school. Your mom and aunt need you, too. You can do this, you hear me? I love you." She hugged Lauren close and could have sworn that the girl's arm touched hers, but it couldn't be true.

Wiping tears away from her face, Elaina left the room and wandered through the corridors until she found Heather and Glenda sitting in a small cafe. Elaina shook her head. "Look, Serena hid the money Charleston, so it's going to take me a few hours to drive each way. When I can confirm the money is there, I will call you so you can make advance arrangements for Lauren's transportation and care. I'll get back as soon as I can. Here's my phone number. Text yours to me." She handed

Glenda a business card and sighed. "I don't know what I'm going to tell Todd, but I'll try to get on the road within the hour."

As Elaina started to leave the room, Glenda grabbed her hand and thanked her one more time. "We're truly blessed to have an angel in our midst. I'm so grateful for your help." Elaina pulled away, gave a slight nod and began twisting her way back to the emergency room waiting area. No matter how sorry Elaina felt for Glenda, she'd never have the warm and fuzzies for her kidnapper. Not only had Glenda put Elaina in grave danger, but she had also stolen her moments of happiness when she should have been celebrating her pregnancy with Todd and the rest of their family.

After leaving Lauren's room, Elaina asked a nurse where she needed to go to be seen by a doctor. She followed their directions, weaving her way to the gynecology and obstetrics floor, where an ultrasound tech told her to lie down. Elaina held her breath and tried not to cry. Had the babies been through too much stress so early in her pregnancy? Would they be okay?

The technician smiled. "Your twins are doing great. They're doing little somersaults right now. That probably explains the pain. Take a look."

Elaina stared at the monitor in awe, sad that Todd wasn't in the room to take in the wonder with her. They'd been through so much together. Hopefully, he was getting some rest. She filled out some paperwork, and the technician told her a doctor would stop by momentarily to answer her questions. After a quick confirmation that the babies' overexertion had caused her stomach discomfort, the doctor recommended that Elaina follow up with her regular doctor.

Todd was still asleep. He looked so adorable and peaceful that Elaina hated to disturb him. She sat down next to this remarkable man and started crafting an elaborate story about why she needed to go to South Carolina. But her stomach knotted, telling her she couldn't lie. Elaina was tired of fighting for her life, but she had to worry about two other little lives now. Protecting the twins was her main goal in life. Being a mom was frightening. You had so much to lose. She'd seen it when her sister, Blake's little girl had gone missing last year. Everything had worked out in the end, but she would never forget the look on Blake's face while they'd waited for her niece to be found. There had been an emptiness to her expression, as if all hope had drained out of her heart.

When Elaina had gathered her thoughts, she woke Todd. Coming out of his groggy state, he seemed to be a little surprised by his surroundings. "Are you okay? Are the babies okay?"

She nodded and embraced him. "Babe, I need a huge favor, and we should probably go pick up Clint because we're probably going to need the Charleston Police Department on our side. I'll explain on the way." *This should be interesting.*

His eyes widened. "Should I be worried?

Elaina shook her head. "For the first time in three weeks, there isn't a single thing for you to worry about, but I need to help a friend. It's complicated but not illegal per se. Taking Clint with us is like having homeowner's insurance. You sure hope you never need it, but if you do, you'll be glad that you took out a policy."

Todd grinned and squeezed her hand. "Whatever you need." *That was much easier than expected!* Relieved, Elaina texted Clint to tell him to get ready to leave for an impromptu car trip to Charleston. She was counting on her brother-in-law to help explain their family's history with the paranormal to Todd. Hopefully, that explanation would make it easier for him to understand how Elaina had become entangled with Glenda's family.

21

The three-hour drive down the coast to Charleston seemed to fly by. Seeing the expansive Arthur Ravenel suspension bridge off in the distance made the strange mission seem more real. Elaina's stomach gurgled and flip-flopped as Todd drove over the uneven ballast stone streets in the historic district. Clutching her abdomen, she tried to calm her nerves, focusing on the lush greenery and red bows that decorated the gas lamps.

When Todd parked along the Battery, he turned to look at Elaina, who had ridden in the backseat. "Babe, I know you've mentioned that your family has a sixth sense, but you've never wanted to talk about it. So, let me make sure I understand properly—you see ghosts. Because you are pregnant with twins, you've developed a special power to see the memories of dead people." He paused and stared at Elaina, and she nodded.

"I know it's insane." Maybe they had found their way into Wonderland. It would be more plausible than the so-called reality.

He looked up at the roof of the Jeep and rubbed his temples before starting again. "Glenda is the sister of one of the ghosts, um, ghost mermaids you banished last year, and now, we're going to stick our heads down inside cannons to see if the ghost mermaid left money inside one of them before she died? This sounds very normal." He rubbed his nose and grinned.

Elaina scrunched up her face and giggled. "It sounds crazy when you say it aloud all at once, but yep, that pretty much sums it up." Geez, this wasn't your average road trip. Couldn't her family have just one milestone or trip without a ghost being involved? Probably not. At least they'd become accustomed to having extra baggage of the supernatural variety.

Swallowing a sip of coffee, Clint held up his index finger and cleared his throat. "Since you haven't been around for our past haunted house adventures, there's one more part you need to be aware of. Because you love Elaina, you share her powers. It's a way of allowing you to protect your significant other. Their Granny Mason explained it to me a long time ago, and it's been true for Ryan and me. I never believed in this spooky stuff before getting back together with Blake, but it's legit. And, believe it or not, I'm glad I can see these things. I wouldn't want her to feel alone in it, especially now that we have a kid. Plus, I've been able to see my grandma pretty often since she died. How many people can say that?"

Clint looked down at his athletic shoes. His beloved grandmother, Nancy, had raised him and his brothers after their parents died in a horrific car accident. Six years ago, the vengeful spirit of Blake's ex-fiancé, Parker, had killed Nancy to punish Blake for leaving him and reuniting with Clint. But the Nelson sisters and their Granny Mason had sent him packing. And after Macy was born, Nancy's ghost had made a welcome return, helping the Nelson sisters ward off evil more than once.

Todd's smile vanished, and he slapped Clint on the back. "Man, it's easy to forget how much this family has been through sometimes. Thank God these Nelson women are as tough as nails."

"Amen to that, brother," Clint said, ruffling Elaina's hair.

Her brother-in-law was a dependable presence in her family's lives. They never had to question his loyalty to Blake or that he loved their little girl, Macy. What's more, he selflessly showed up anytime the Nelson sisters or their parents needed anything.

Overcome with emotion, she hugged Clint and motioned for Todd to join them. After she let go, she stood back and smiled at them. "Thanks so much for coming to help me with this weird mission. Lauren is super important to me. She was sweet to me the whole time I was there, and she was the one who helped me get away." She sniffed. "Now, she might die. I can't imagine being a kid and going through everything she has."

Todd tilted his head, and his gaze softened. "Lauren is lucky to have you watching out for her even though her family has endangered you and our unborn children more than once. And as misguided and illegal as her mom and aunt's efforts were, it sounds like they care about her deeply."

"They love her. I feel awful for all of them, despite everything." Elaina pushed back the tears that stung her eyes. "Okay. How do we go about retrieving a fanny pack full of money from the depths of a cannon?" What a bizarre thing to say! She and Todd both turned to look at Clint at the same time.

"Why are you guys looking at me? Just because I've lived here my entire life? You've gotta be kidding me! I wouldn't have ever dared to hide something inside one of these cannons. My grandma would have wrung my neck for sure, or, at the very least, she would have made me pick a switch for a whooping. You know how she was. We were taught not to touch things that weren't ours. I'm trying to teach Macy to be just as respectful."

Elaina shrugged. "But Nancy didn't know everything you did as a kid."

"Did I hear someone say my name?" a familiar voice asked. Elaina squinted and looked up to see Clint hugging Nancy, who was standing beside one of the massive black cannons.

Todd's eyes widened just before he nodded in Nancy's direction. "So that's Clint's dead grandmother, and she's here to help us look for something Serena hid in a cannon in the 1980s?"

Elaina laughed. "Yep. That's right. You'll love Nancy if you talk to her. There's nothing to be afraid of—I promise!"

She ran over to her ghostly friend. "When did you get here? Where did you come from? Have you seen Granny Mason?" Nancy had been Granny's best friend in life, and nothing had changed in the afterlife. These two always said they were "as thick as thieves." What a funny Southern colloquialism.

Nanny smiled. "Hon, I came to help you as soon as I could. I promise we'll sit down and catch up as soon as we get your friend squared away. So, do you have any clue which cannon Serena stashed the purse inside?"

"Good question." Elaina tried to imagine her dream and walked through Serena's steps to hide her fanny pack. Playing back Serena's memory, Elaina found something that she'd missed the first time around–raw emotion and anxiety. In life, Serena must have been terrified, carrying around a large sum of money and not having a way to keep it safe. Of course, she didn't have any way of knowing that she was going to die the very night when she'd hidden the fanny pack. Pulling herself out of the depths of Serena's emotions, Elaina focused on remembering the factual side of the events that had taken place.

As Serena carefully packed her bag into the gun, the sweeping Spanish moss whirled in the wind, and the blue water behind the seawall sparkled. *That's it!* Elaina shook herself out of the trance. "Hey, y'all! It has to be one of the ones on the East side of the Battery, facing the seawall!" She ran over to a cannon and looked down inside. "Do you have a flashlight? I can't see a damn thing!"

Todd opened the tailgate of the Jeep and grabbed a couple of flashlights from the bed. He tossed one to Clint, and they each took the cannon closest to them. Elaina watched each of them staring down their respective gun's deep chamber. She couldn't stand just watching them, but there wasn't anything else that she could do.

Clint motioned for her to come over and join him. "So, I see a lot of leaves, dead palmetto bugs and, I'm pissed off about this part—ice cream wrappers. The nerve of these effin tourists! But at any rate, there's definitely not a fanny pack or any other purse. Want to see for yourself?"

"No, that's okay. I trust you. Actually, yeah, I will, but only because I'm curious what the inside of a cannon looks like."

He nodded and pointed the flashlight's beam down the gun. Elaina stood on her tiptoes and peeked inside. Looking past the disgusting debris Clint had mentioned, Elaina felt a cold chill tingle down her back as she examined the artifact in front of her. This is the reason Charleston was so special. History was everywhere, including Serena's.

Hopefully, Todd was having more luck. Mere feet away, he was digging inside the cannon with a long tree branch, scraping globs of sludge out of the relic's interior. "This is disgusting, not that I expected them to be spotless. Just know I love you."

Elaina kissed his cheek. "I love you and appreciate what everyone is doing to help. I'm very grateful. Do you see anything that resembles a purse down in there?"

He shook his head. "Not yet, at least, but I'm not ready to throw in the towel." It had to be down in there. If it wasn't, there were at least seven or eight more cannons in the park. Maybe she and Nancy should start checking them.

"Hey, Nancy. I don't think this is the case, but I could have been wrong about which cannon she left the money inside. Do you want to look inside the ones on the other side of the park?"

Her friend materialized on the West end of the empty gardens without saying a word and began her in-depth search. The spirit's approach to looking inside the cannon differed from both of the guys' simple tactics. She walked through the barrel from one end to the other, placing her head inside the chamber and look around. At moments, it appeared that she was wearing the cannon as a bulky iron skirt, and at others, a strange headpiece. *What a weird thing to witness!*

After a few minutes, Elaina tore herself away from watching Nancy and began investigating the interior of one of the shorter-barreled guns. The built-in flashlight in her cell phone provided just enough glow. The interior of this one had been partially filled with concrete, and the remaining portion of the barrel was remarkably clean compared to the others, not an ice cream wrapper in sight.

A ladybug landed on her arm, but she could hardly complain about its presence. These creatures were supposed to bring good luck to those who crossed their paths. She needed all the good luck she could find. Nothing could have been hidden in the depths of this cannon, so Elaina stood upright and scanned the park for her family.

Everyone else was standing back beside the car, looking defeated. She ran over to them and sighed. "No one had any luck at all?"

Todd leaned forward and placed his hand on her arm. "Is there a chance she wasn't in Charleston or at least not in the Battery when she hid the money?"

Elaina shook her head. "No. She hid the money here. I know that for a fact."

Clint's eyes widened. "Then, someone has moved the money, but who and where did they move it to? Is there anyone she may have told about the money? I mean other than her sisters unless you think one of them took it and didn't want the other one to know."

"I really don't think they would do that to each other, and from what I know about Serena, she didn't trust anyone. She wouldn't have shared something so important with anyone other than her family."

What was the answer, then? Had someone found the money and stashed it in a new spot? It was unlikely. Decades had passed since the money had been hidden. There would have been news coverage and gossip around some honest person finding a large sum of money, especially inside a cannon! Granny Mason and Nancy would have remembered such a notable story. Wouldn't they? It wouldn't hurt to ask.

"Hey, Nancy, do you remember hearing any stories about city employees or preservationists finding thousands of dollars inside a cannon or anywhere else downtown?"

Her spirited friend shook her head. "Nope. This is the first time I've ever heard of such a thing. That type of news definitely would have gotten around, and you know when I worked at the Sea Biscuit, my customers kept me pretty well informed." Very true. The residents of Isle of Palms had seen Nancy as a surrogate grandmother. Many had gone to the small island diner to see her whenever they needed advice or wanted to share a juicy rumor. At least half of the island's residents attended her funeral to pay their respects.

Elaina sighed. How was she going to help Lauren if they couldn't find the money? If she had one of Serena's earthly possessions, she could have tried to use her newfound powers to dig through the mermaid spirit's memories again. But Elaina didn't have so much as one of Serena's scrunchies.

Nancy squeezed Elaina's hand. "You know what you're gonna have to do, hon. It's not gonna be pretty, but we don't have much of a choice."

Elaina's stomach churned. Why did Nancy always have to be right?

22

The sky changed from a brilliant blue to a dark gray, and the wind coming off the seawall sliced through Elaina's jacket. December weather in the Lowcountry was hit or miss. One day could be 85 degrees, and the next 35. Go figure, the one day that Elaina needed clear weather would be the nastiest.

Of course, winter storms made all the difference in temperature drops. Christmastime tornadoes and hail storms had become a new normal in the South. Before Nancy died, she blamed the lousy weather on greedy people who had forgotten the true meaning of Christmas. She always said this was God's way of punishing people for focusing on the commercialized side.

Todd helped Elaina get into the Jeep and covered her with a blanket. "Are you sure you want to do this, babe? No one would blame you for giving up after the money wasn't where Serena had left it. You did your best to help the kid, and I love you for it. We all do, but you're not in the best shape to run all over the place and put yourself into these hazardous situations. We have our own family to consider now."

He kissed her hand and placed it on her stomach. Elaina's heart sank. He wasn't wrong, but not doing something when a child was suffering wasn't right either. She had to help, even if it was risky, not to mention plain terrifying.

Before Elaina could respond, a text notification came through on her phone. She didn't have to check the screen to know the text was coming from Glenda.

Glenda: Hey, good and bad news–Lauren isn't out of the woods, but her doctor said she is in stable enough condition to be airlifted to Nashville. The bad news is that the specialist is leaving the country for six months in a couple of weeks. So, if we don't scrape the money together by tomorrow night, we won't be able to get her there in time. Have you had any luck?

Elaina: It wasn't in the location I saw in Serena's dream, but don't worry yet. I have another plan.

Glenda: I don't know how to thank you, and I know I shouldn't say this, but please hurry!

The phone dropped out of Elaina's hand, crashing onto the floorboard. With her already frayed nerves standing on end, she did the only thing she could—close her eyes and scream. Blood pulsed through her veins, and her lungs felt more open than they had in months, which made sense. She had lifted the proverbial weight off her chest.

Todd put the Jeep back into park and turned to look at Elaina. "Babe, what in the hell is wrong? Are you okay? Do you need to see a doctor?"

She shook her head. "Nope. I'm fine, just feeling a ton of pressure to get this right. We have to go to Sweetgrass Island right now. There's no time to waste."

His green eyes narrowed. "Let's at least go to Clint and Blake's house so you can lie down for a few minutes and eat something. Before you argue with me, I just want to point out that it would help you feel better."

Elaina resisted the urge to scream again. Taking a deep breath, she simply shook her head. "We have to go now, or it's going to be too late." She shot Todd a sharp look, and Clint laughed.

"Your sister makes the same look when she's angry. I've learned she means business when I see it on her face. Brother, you'd best put the pedal to the metal. On second thought, let me drive."

Todd and Clint jumped out of the Jeep and quickly traded places. After Clint adjusted the driver's seat and mirrors, he pushed a button on the dash and grinned.

"What does that do?" Elaina asked, leaning forward to examine the unmarked piece of gray plastic.

"Um, it makes things a lot easier." He peered up at the rearview mirror and winked at Elaina. When blue lights reflected on the wet pavement, she grinned. Being related to the police chief had its advantages. When Clint sped up, the contents of her stomach sloshed around, and she questioned these so-called benefits.

"Easy there, speedy!" Elaina slapped him on the back. "We're in a hurry, but don't forget that I'm pregnant. I don't want to barf all over your backseat."

Clint laughed. "I'll dial it back a notch."

"Whew! I hope so! The three of us thank you!"

Todd turned and stared at her. "I know you've been through hell lately, but I haven't told you how beautiful you are. Being pregnant agrees with you, other than the pukey part at least." She smiled. Maybe they'd get to celebrate their growing family during the upcoming holiday festivities properly.

A green road sign caught Elaina's eye—two miles to the Isle of Palms Marina. Hopefully, she'd remember Brittany's description of getting to their exact destination once they arrived on the island. What if she didn't? This was her last shot at finding out where the money ended up, and if it didn't work out, what would happen to Lauren?

"Nancy? Are you with us?" Elaina called out. Nancy had been with her last year during the life-changing events that had taken place. Death had somehow sharpened her memory and other faculties ... one of the bonuses of the afterlife. A silvery glow revealed itself next to Elaina, and Nancy's spirit slowly appeared. *Thank God!*

"What did you need, hon? Are you feeling okay? I was trying to find your granny. She's been with your papa on the Other Side. It gets harder to come back every time I go there. I can see why she stayed, well, and the love of her life is there. I don't have that special person waiting for me. I mean, my parents and some of my sisters are there, but I feel more drawn to my earthly family, my boys and my grandbabies."

Elaina had missed Granny Mason. She made a mental note to ask Nancy more questions about her grandparents' where-abouts, but for now, she needed her friend's help to figure out where they needed to go next.

"Did Granny mention how to get to where we're going? I'd text Brittany, but she's still out of town at an architecture conference."

"Of course, silly. Why else would I bother Julia Caroline Mason in Paradise? You should see her. She is positively radi-ant, in fact. Your grandfather can't take his eyes off her. I'm so happy for them."

Elaina couldn't stop the tears in her eyes from falling. What a lovely description of her grandparents, whose beautiful love story was famous around the island. They'd kept their romance alive even after death. That's all anyone could ask for. No wonder Granny Mason had wanted to cross over for good. Life on earth as a spirit would pale in comparison in every way.

Pulling herself together, Elaina wiped away the salty tears from her cheeks and smiled at Nancy. "Pregnancy hormones are a bitch."

"It was a long time ago for me, but I seem to remember something about that. Anyway, I hope you didn't think I aban-doned you. I just wanted to make sure we'd be able to find what we're after."

Elaina nodded. "I'm glad you did." The Nelson sisters were fortunate to have a supportive family, including Nancy, looking out for them. She'd always treated them as her own grandchildren, and they couldn't love her more. Of course, Granny Mason had lucked out having Nancy as her best friend, too. They're unfaltering connection had seen them through complicated situations on earth and beyond the grave.

There was one loose end Elaina from her grandmother's memories that she wanted to tie up. Unfortunately, there wasn't time to dive into the past to see it play out firsthand. Maybe Nancy would have the answer. "Hey, I've been meaning to ask you or Granny—what happened to Great Grandpa Mason? Did he stay on the Other Side? Did y'all ever have to fight him again?" Elaina shivered.

Nancy shook her head. "That spirit stayed put. Thank goodness. I don't think poor Julia Caroline or James could have handled dealing with any more crap from him. He was a handful."

Elaina breathed a sigh of relief. Her grandparents had been able to start their marriage without an evil spirit in tow. Hopefully, Elaina and Todd would be able to do the same.

23

Once they arrived at the marina, Elaina ran over to Clint's boat. Walking around, she didn't see his diving gear locker sitting in its usual spot. "Hey, where are your wetsuits, diving tanks and masks?"

Todd put out his hand. "I don't know what you're looking for, but you're not diving for anything, especially not in this freezing cold water. You've put yourself in too much danger as it is. Tell us what you need, and we'll go get it."

"But you don't have my abilities, you won't know which shark to look for, and even if you did, you wouldn't be able to undo the bottling spell to release Serena."

"What in the hell are you talking about? Tell me exactly why you've brought us here and what it has to do with a shark and a spell? I know you can see ghosts, but you're not a witch? Are you?"

Elaina explained how just a year ago, she and her sisters had captured the mermaid spirit and banished her to the belly of a shark. If they hadn't, Serena would have killed them and forced them to be part of her underwater army for all eternity.

Todd's eyes widened, and the color drained from his face.

"Like I said earlier, I don't think I fully appreciated what your family has been through. I think I need to sit down for a minute." Elaina felt horrible. She'd never meant to drag Todd into her family's paranormal nightmare. Now, she realized she had made a mistake in not sharing more about their gifts and the horrors they'd faced.

"I'm sorry I didn't tell you all of this last year. I didn't know where to start. I never thought you would be involved in any of this. That was wishful thinking. I mean, Clint has been dragged through hell and back with Blake several times, and Ryan dealt with more than his share of the shit show last year. I guess I should have known your turn to face our family's demons would come due."

Nancy stepped forward and smiled at Todd. "What you need to know is that the Nelson sisters can take care of themselves. And they don't need guns or knives to take care of business. They just know what to do. It's in their blood."

Footsteps outside the boat got Elaina's attention, and she looked up to see Granny Mason standing on the dock. A warm sensation pulsed through Elaina's body. Granny had left the beautiful afterlife with her one true love to support her family yet again. This selfless matriarch always put her granddaughters' lives at the top of her priorities.

"Granny? You came! But Nancy said you looked so happy with Papa. Why would you give that up?" Elaina embraced her grandmother in awe.

Pulling away, Granny Mason held Elaina's hands firmly. "Sweetie, you know I'll always find a way to be with you girls. I told you that before I died. I meant that. I know I said I needed to be with your grandfather, but I told him I couldn't stay away from my family when y'all need me. I'm grateful Nancy came to tell me what was going on. I want to be here with you."

Up until now, Todd had seemed to deal with Nancy's presence, and the ghost talk pretty well. Perhaps he hadn't taken the subject matter seriously. But the look in his eyes as he stared at

Granny Mason told Elaina everything she needed to know about how he felt right now.

"It's like I told you about Nancy — there's no reason to be afraid. We don't have time to get into a deep philosophical conversation right now, but yes, this is my dead grandmother, Julia Caroline Mason, aka Granny Mason. She left her posh afterlife with my grandfather to help us get through the next part of finding the money for Lauren. I know my life is insanely weird, but I promise we've made it through similar predicaments. Strange situations are always easier with Granny Mason and Nancy around."

Todd rubbed his temples. "I'm so sorry I haven't been around more to support you while your family has gone through all this crap. I know I've let my job take the forefront in my life quite a bit, but I promise to find a better balance and be around when you need me."

Granny Mason winked. "It's so great knowing all of my granddaughters found men like my husband. I have a lot more peace when I'm away from y'all."

Elaina smiled. "I love all of you, and we'll take lots of time to celebrate as soon as we've talked to Serena and given that sea witch a one-way ticket back to the belly of the shark. Now, c'mon! We've gotta get to Sweetgrass Island already!" Elaina shifted the boat into drive, and Clint offered to take over so she could sit with Todd, who still looked a little stunned. *Poor guy!*

Plopping down next to Todd, Elaina leaned on his shoulder. "Thank you for being with me, not just now, but in life. I can't wait to do all the normal couple things like plan a wedding and raise these wonderful babies with you." As the saltwater gently misted Elaina's face, her heart raced at the thought of all these special moments that were on the horizon for them. The future held so much promise. Hopefully, she'd be able to give Lauren the same chance at a full life.

<<<<<<<<<<<>>>>>>>>>>>

Approaching the familiar dock, where all hell had broken loose just a year ago, gave Elaina some pause about her decision to visit Sweetgrass Island again. She rubbed her arms. Was it a good idea to come back? Were they in danger? The live oaks beckoned them to step on dry land, just like an old friend sitting on a rocking chair on their front porch. Strands of Spanish moss whipped in the wind, and the birds called out a melodic tune. She gulped but helped Todd moor the boat. They'd come too far for a very important cause to turn back now.

Nancy and Granny Mason appeared on the shoreline, making it easier for Elaina to prepare for the impending challenges mentally. Knowing she had these strong women on her side, they could easily take on the shark, Serena and anything else that came next.

Todd stepped up onto the dock first and offered Elaina a hand. "Don't hate me, but I have to ask one more time. Are you sure you want to do this? I'm just worried about you and the babies."

"For the billionth time, I'm positive. One day, our kids could be in trouble. Wouldn't you want someone to step up and protect them however possible?"

"Of course, but I also want to protect them and you right now. But if you tell me you've got this, I'll step out of your way because I love you."

Elaina nodded. "I've got this. I love you, too. Now, I want to get this over with so we can help Lauren as soon as possible."

Clint brought three sets of diving gear off the boat. "I thought all three of us could go to help keep your mind at ease, Todd. That way, you're not just watching from the surface wondering what's going on down there."

"Thanks, bro. Listen to me, Elaina." *Yikes! He never calls me by my first name!* "If things go sideways, you'd better be ready to bail. The four of us will take care of whatever happens. Right everyone?"

The two ghostly matriarchs and Clint nodded in unison, and Todd's upright posture softened slightly. Elaina felt bad for him. All of this stress couldn't be good for his blood pressure. Within just a few weeks, he'd been concerned about Elaina's health, found out she was pregnant with twins, she had been kidnapped, and she'd escaped. Now, they were trying to pull off a seemingly impossible task involving an evil mermaid spirit and a dangerous shark. It was a lot for the average person to take in at one time.

Pulling on her wetsuit, she thought of ways she could pay Todd back for everything she'd put him through over the past couple of weeks. During the upcoming Christmas holiday break, she'd make sure he played his favorite board games, drink Irish coffee and read by the fireplace. Maybe they could take a short babymoon trip to celebrate the New Year. Assuming they made it out of the potentially harrowing interaction with Serena unscathed.

fter everyone had put on their gear, one by one, they jumped into the Intracoastal waterway, following Granny Mason and Nancy through the seagrass beds. Taking in the underwater environment, Elaina thanked her father for insisting that she and her sisters take diving lessons.

He'd wanted his daughters to be well-rounded in every way, and mostly, he'd gotten his wish. Blake was a writer who owned and managed a bed and breakfast; Brittany was an architect and mentor for deaf children wanting to go to college, and Elaina's banking career had been on the rise since she'd started, and it didn't show any sign of slowing down. Soon, Elaina would add another role to her resume, one that both of her sisters had successfully achieved—mother.

Coming back to the task at hand, Elaina noticed a makeshift cavern just ahead. The crumbling pilings matched Brittany's description; this had to be the place. Clint focused an underwater flashlight on the opening, which was blocked by a large boulder. How on earth would they move that huge sucker? The guys tried pushing the rock, but it barely budged and rolled back into its starting point. *Geez. Great. What now?* Todd grabbed a flat dinner plate-sized stone, slid it into a gap, trying to pry the boulder out of the entryway. It moved a few inches, but certainly not enough for anyone, including the shark, to get through.

Granny Mason motioned for everyone to move away, and she grabbed one of Nancy's hands. They closed their eyes and pointed toward the cavern entrance. Although Elaina couldn't hear the words her grandmother and friend were reciting, she knew they must have a bit of magic up their figurative sleeves. A bright beam shot out of each of the matriarch spirits' free hands. The same type of light had streamed from her granny's hands during past battles against evil spirits. Would it work against such a densely heavy object? At first, nothing happened. Elaina closed her eyes and prayed for a miracle. Drawing a deep, cleansing breath, she opened her eyes to see the massive boulder roll aside. *Thank goodness!*

The group slowly swam into the cavern. Elaina had to resist the urge to scream when she saw three sharks baring their pointy teeth while circling a rock formation. How could they figure out which fish housed the mermaid army? Last year, Granny Mason and Brittany had trapped two sharks in the cavern, so they'd reproduce. When the elder shark died, its spirit would transfer the mermaid army to its offspring. One of the sharks was clearly the youngest, but what about the other two?

Elaina motioned to the larger sharks and shrugged, hoping her grandmother would remember. Granny Mason pointed to a shimmering pink mark in the shape of a conch shell on the stomach of one of the older sharks. *Aha!* It should have been evident to her earlier. At any rate, what came next? They probably needed to separate the host shark from its family, but how could they safely do that?

Clint pointed to his wrist, indicating they should start

ascending toward the boat, but they weren't even close to being done with the shark. Elaina couldn't speak underwater, unlike the ghostly women, so everyone needed to surface to help reverse the bottling spell. As usual, Granny Mason read her mind and motioned for her to leave the underwater abyss.

The ascent gave Elaina plenty of time to think about what would happen next. She trusted her grandmother more than anyone in the world and knew she had a brilliant plan in the works. So what was up with the heart palpitations? *Should I worry? No! This isn't the time. Having a panic attack underwater is a terrible idea!* Focusing only on the bubbles coming out of her mask, she calmed her heart rate and steadied her breathing pattern.

The brackish water transformed from deep blue to a lighter gray, and the surface was finally in sight. *What a relief!* When Elaina finally broke through, Granny Mason and Nancy were floating on the surface, hovering over the shark, which seemed to be intoxicated by their charms. Giggling at the sight, Elaina struggled to climb the boat's swim ladder, but she made it onto the deck on the second try. Clint and Todd ascended from the depths of the waterway soon afterward and climbed onto the watercraft.

"Alright, we're ready," Elaina said, clasping her hands together. "Granny, what do we need to do?"

"I know it was Brittany's battle to fight last year, but do you remember the words for reversing the bottling spell?"

Elaina nodded and fist-pumped. "Release Serena from her watery cell, give her freedom. Bring her back from this hell." Her heart raced again, but this time, it wasn't anxiety driven. She felt empowered, strong for the first time since being kidnapped.

When Granny Mason and Nancy joined her on the boat deck, the shark stayed in its place. The women joined hands and, in unison, repeated the short incantation three times. Rays of light shot out of the shark, like eight laser beams, briefly blinding Elaina. Her vision normalized just in time to see that the sassy sea witch had returned in all of her 1980s glory, wearing a flawless hot pink business suit and black lace gloves.

Serena placed her hands on her hips. "So, like, what in the hell did you do to me? I'm going to totally murder you!"

Todd jumped in front of Elaina and waved his arms. "You'd better leave her alone. She's been busting her ass just to save your niece. Now, shut your effing mouth and listen to what she has to say." Elaina's jaw dropped. This type of outburst was uncharacteristic for her normally passive husband-to-be.

"Niece? I don't have a niece. And you shut up, or I'll make sure you end up just like my favorite kind of tea—in a bag, underwater." Serena chomped on a wad of watermelon-scented gum and blew a bubble. Despite having been immersed in the paranormal world for six years, Elaina still had a mind-boggling number of questions. How did bubble gum survive decades of being underwater, not to mention in a ghost's possession, while she lived inside a shark?

"Like the man said. Shut up, Serena." Elaina smirked. "You have a 14-year-old niece named Lauren. She's Glenda's daughter, and she's sick. Your sisters have done everything they can to get treatments for her. Your memories of hiding your money in a cannon were totally off base, so where did you leave the cash?"

Serena twirled her hair around her index finger. "Wait. Why would you want to help them? That doesn't, like, make any sense." Of course, the narcissistic spirit wouldn't understand why someone would do something kind for a stranger.

"Glenda didn't give me much of a choice. She kidnapped me and forced me to use some of my abilities to go into your memories, only I guess I didn't see the one where you moved the money from the cannon to a new location. So, tell me where it is now."

"Why didn't Glenda or Heather come tell me themselves?" Serena pouted, staring off into the distance.

Elaina narrowed her eyes. "You really can't grasp that you're not the most important part of this equation. Lauren is going to die if you don't give them the money for her treatment. I know when you were alive, you intended to give the money to your sisters. Don't keep it away from them now just to spite me. This really has nothing to do with me, but I got to know your niece, and I love her. I don't want anything to happen to an innocent kid. Please try to find a bit of compassion to help her."

Serena sat down on the boat and wailed. If this had been Elaina's first time seeing a spirit, she would have freaked out hearing the mermaid ghost's cry, which was pretty much the universal spooky haunted house ghost sound.

Momentarily, Todd's face went as white as a sheet. He gave Elaina a pointed look, and she shook her head. "She'll be fine. Don't worry." Mostly, the color returned to his cheeks, but the worry in his eyes was still apparent when he embraced Elaina as if to protect her from Serena's outburst. Elaina placed her hands on Todd's arms and looked up at him. "Seriously, it will be okay. Sure, she's unhinged, but I have Granny and Nancy with me."

"Don't talk about me like I'm not here!" Serena screamed. "I'll show you unhinged!" The sea witch pointed her hands at Elaina, sending her spiraling out of the boat and at least 20 feet into the air. Stomach churning, Elaina screamed as she plunged toward the water, stopping just inches away from the water and hovering over the surface.

Facing the lapping waves, Elaina knew it was just a matter of time before the tide came in, forcing its icy cold slush into her lungs. "Granny! Nancy! Y'all, I need some help right now!"

Serena cackled. "They're a little busy right now, making sure the boat doesn't sink with Blake's lover boy on it. P.S. It's not looking so great for Clint. He'll make a great addition to my army."

Elaina had to do something quickly, but what? She could see and communicate with spirits, but she wasn't a witch. The spells her family knew were ones they'd read in books. If her phone was within reach, she might find an incantation that would help, but it could take a while. Maybe her phone was the answer, though.

"Hey, Serena, if you put me back on the boat, I can prove to you that Lauren is your niece, and she needs your help."

The mermaid spirit bit her lip and folded her arms over her chest. "I don't see how, but what's the harm in letting you live for a few more minutes?"

As Elaina's body floated upward and toward the boat, she breathed a sigh of relief, but her calmness faded when she saw her family struggling to keep the watercraft afloat. Realizing she might push her luck, she asked, "Can you maybe stop trying to sink the boat for a hot minute, too?"

Serena rolled her eyes and grunted. "Whatever. Okay. Now, make this quick. Show me this so-called proof that you have that I'm an aunt."

Elaina's fingers trembled as she pulled out her cell phone to place a video call to Glenda. "Hey, I'm here with Serena. I know you can't see or hear her, but can you please tell her why you need the money?" Elaina handed her phone to the mermaid spirit and watched her face fall as Glenda shared the tragic story of Lauren's illness and how she was on the verge of death, but the doctors believed that one specific treatment might save the child. Serena sat in silence, wiping a tear from her fuchsia rouge-covered cheek.

She handed the phone back to Elaina. "Tell her I'll help you find the money right now. I won't mess around anymore. I promise."

For a moment, Elaina almost felt bad for Serena, but after everything the sea witch had put them through over the past couple of years, the feeling faded. But it didn't matter. They had the same goal now—to help Lauren survive. That's all that mattered.

"So, where do we need to go to get the money? Please tell me you remember where you moved it to."

"Of course I do, but it won't be easy to get there." Serena explained that the day before she died, she heard that the city of Charleston was planning to restore the cannons at White Point Gardens. Understandably, she'd panicked and started brainstorming new locations where no one was likely to look.

"That's when I decided no one would ever find the money inside good Ol' Rusty."

Elaina blinked. Old Rusty was the nickname for the decommissioned Sweetgrass Island Lighthouse, which was now surrounded by water. No one could get inside except for the Isle of Palms Police Department, the Coast Guard and a handful of trusted restoration organization leaders.

"How on earth did you manage that?"

"At the time, I was dating and living with a retired Coast Guard officer. Early one morning, I *borrowed* his keys and boat and hid the money inside a hidden panel in one of the window panes. It was a frightening experience because, well, you know how choppy the water is there. I nearly destroyed my boyfriend's boat more than once during that excursion, and I almost drowned when I got into the lighthouse. The stairs were slick. Somehow, I slipped the fanny pack down into the panel without breaking my neck. I remember regretting my decision to hide the money there that day, but thinking back, I don't think I could have chosen a better spot. I don't see how anyone could have found my stash."

"Very true. Do you think that you can stop trying to kill us long enough to go look for the money and get it to your sisters?"

Serena twisted her mouth. "I think I can do that."

"Great! Now, let's get going." Elaina turned to Clint. "Do you know how to get into the lighthouse?"

Fiddling with his keyring, Clint held up a scratched-up bronze key. "Um, I've never been in there, but we can try."

When they pulled up alongside the lighthouse, the water swelled and slammed against the white brick exterior. Elaina gasped as the waves took a cluster of oysters with them as they retreated. *Oh, God. What have we gotten ourselves into? How can we get inside without the undertow drowning us or our bodies being beaten to a bloody pulp against the bricks?*

25

Both Clint and Todd had lived near the Atlantic Ocean their entire lives and had plenty of experience dealing with currents. They knew better than to just jump into the water, even if it appeared to be relatively shallow. So, the two of them devised a plan to cross the gap between the boat and the decaying lighthouse steps. Elaina smiled as she watched them draw diagrams and ransack the hold like children going through a toy chest.

Grinning ear to ear, Todd set down boards, life preservers, rope and a bucket full of rock climbing gear near the aft of the watercraft. "Thank goodness Clint has a big boat and, apparently, hoarding tendencies."

"Hey, watch it. If I didn't keep stuff longer than *some* people, we'd be screwed right now." Clint winked at Elaina.

Elaina had to laugh. These guys had reverted to their childhood, but she was glad Todd got along with both of her sisters' husbands. It certainly made life easier during good times and the bad, and in this family, the line between the two often blurred. At least they had each other.

Clint inflated his dinghy before throwing the anchor down

into the depths and tossing the small boat into the water immediately afterward. "Okay, guys. I know this sounds crazy, but here's the plan. I'm gonna try to jump into the dingy from here. If the water is smooth enough, I'll tie it off at the railing. If things go sideways, I'm gonna need you to get creative. You have a mixture of crap that you can use however it makes sense."

"Be careful. Blake won't ever forgive me if you get hurt." Elaina punched him in the shoulder.

Clint pretended like he was going to push Elaina overboard, but she knew better. Rolling her eyes, she shooed him. "Whatever, dude. Just go. Let's get this over with."

Her brother-in-law shrugged and took a running jump, shaking the entire boat. Todd cheered him on, but Elaina covered her eyes with her hand.

"I can't watch!" *Gah! Please let him make it!*

"Yeah, yeah! Who's da man?" Clint yelled. Taking his proclamation as a good sign, Elaina peeked through her fingers to see her brother-in-law kneeling in the dinghy. *Thank God!*

The small boat seemed to handle the waves pretty well from Elaina's vantage point; Clint must have agreed because he started the troller, taking him the rest of the way. After he tied off at the railing, he jumped onto the top step and grabbed his keys. Opening the door to the lighthouse, Clint looked back at Elaina and Todd with widened eyes. "We're in! Okay, Serena, I need you to show me the money. Sorry, I've always wanted to say that. Take me wherever you stashed the cash back in the '80s."

Serena glared at Elaina. "Is he always this corny? Wait, don't answer that. I remember from my last run-in with your fam. Like, gag me with a spoon." After pretending to shove her finger down her throat, she floated from the boat to the lighthouse's interior. Before following her inside, Granny Mason and Nancy stopped to talk to Elaina.

Nancy grimaced. "I don't trust that sea witch any further

than I can throw a bushel of fossilized sand dollars. I've gotta keep an eye on my boy."

Granny Mason shushed her. "Nan, you need to calm yourself. I'm not saying I fully disagree, but she ain't worth the fuss you're making. Let's just get in there."

"You hush now, ya hear me, troll?" Nancy stuck out her tongue and glided from the boat to the lighthouse. Granny Mason threw up her hands but calmed herself and made her way across the water.

Elaina shook her head. Nancy and Granny Mason had been best friends their entire lives, apparently, a bond that death couldn't break. But that didn't mean they didn't bicker like "two old wet hens," their words, not Elaina's. It was funny and endearing to listen to her grandmother rein in Nancy before she completely went off the deep end, not that Nancy would let her get in the last word.

Would the Nelson sisters end up being just like them one day? Probably. Usually, the three of them got along, and even if they were slightly annoyed with one another, they understood each other's intentions. Occasionally, though, extreme circumstances brewed the perfect climate for a storm. Both of her sisters thought they knew better than each other. Elaina tried to stay out of their nonsensical arguments, but she wasn't always successful.

Now that everyone had made it into the lighthouse, Elaina could appreciate its rustic beauty and charm. The white brick structure cast its afternoon shadow onto the nearby sand flat. Preservationists had done wonders to keep the centuries-old lighthouse intact, raising money for restoration during special events. She was impressed by all of their hard work to keep the decommissioned light functional as a piece of history for future generations. Someone had even taken the time to hang garland, a wreath and teal bows along the observation deck.

Things seemed almost too quiet. Just when Elaina thought about sending Todd to check on Clint, a beautiful aria echoed from the top of Old Rusty. The soprano voice had to belong to Serena; how ironic—a mermaid was singing a sea shanty in a lighthouse. Maybe Serena would have been an interesting friend before the bitterness of death had taken its toll on her young life. She'd cared enough to hide money for her sisters, not just once but twice. That wasn't a typical activity for most sociopaths.

Todd took Elaina's hand and kissed it. "You seem distant. What are you thinking about? Do you feel okay?"

"Sorry, babe. I didn't mean to be antisocial. I think I'm just exhausted and hungry. I'm going to sleep for a week straight and then eat everything in the pantry when we get home." She stretched and yawned. The whole ordeal had taken its toll on her body; being pregnant with twins probably hadn't helped her feel more energetic.

He grimaced. "I'm so going to say it one more time—I'm frustrated about everything you've been through. I understand Glenda was desperate to help Lauren, but I still can't imagine doing what she and Heather did to you. It pisses me off that they're going to get away with it. Clint thinks you should call the authorities and tell them the whole story now that the flooding has receded, but it's your choice."

"I've thought about it quite a bit. I can't do that to Lauren. She needs her mom and aunt right now," Elaina whispered, hoping to change the subject. Thankfully, Clint emerged from the lighthouse, holding up the famed pink and black alligator skin fanny pack over his head like a pro wrestler showing off the belt they'd just won during a match. She giggled. What a dork—a very sweet, well-meaning dork! She couldn't wait for the twins to meet him. Todd was the love of her life and would be a great, caring dad to their babies. But he wasn't goofy like Clint, who all children flocked to because he was an overgrown kid himself, making him the perfect uncle.

Todd whooped and clapped. "Way to go, bro!" Being around Clint even brought out the fun side of typically serious Todd's personality. Elaina's fiancé was loving, kind and intelligent, but he needed to loosen up. She was grateful the guys got along as well as they did. Brittany's husband, Ryan, fit in perfectly, too.

As Clint started the dingy, it was clear something was wrong. The engine shut off, and one side of the raft began bouncing up and down. Soon, the other side followed, sending Clint from one end of the small boat to the next. *What on earth is happening?* When the dingy appeared to be levitating away from the larger vessel, Elaina knew something magical was afoot.

"Serena, what exactly do you think you're doing to Clint? We're trying to get this money to your family so that Lauren can get her treatments."

The mermaid waved her hand. "Family, shamily. Who needs them? Have they tried to do anything to help me since I died? Nope. Not a damn thing. My army is my family, and if they know what's good for them, they do what I want." Granny Mason motioned for Elaina to distract Serena, who had her back turned to them.

Elaina played along, scratching her head. "Look, I know you died long before Lauren was born, but don't you care that your sisters are hurting right now? And we didn't release your army when we let you out of the shark. So who or what is moving the dingy? I know it hasn't sprouted wings."

"Did you think I would bring my full army with me to the battle at Blake's house last year? No freaking way. I know better than that. Besides, someone had to stay behind and keep our operation rolling in case something went wrong. They've been looking for us but just hadn't quite made it to the cavern where your effing sister and grandmother locked us up."

"Oh, I didn't realize there were even more spineless sea urchins willing to follow you around and be at your beck and call. How pathetic is that?" Watching out of her peripheral vision, Elaina saw Nancy tie up two mermaids with an iridescent, magical rope. Death hadn't taken away her elderly friend's fiery determination. If anything, it had given her back the strength from her youth, making her unstoppable.

"You don't know anything about our underwater world." Serena sneered. "My army loves me. I've given them a better life after death than they had while they were living. They have a purpose, home and each other. Most of these sad misfits didn't have any of that when they worked for me at the hotel before it burned to the ground. They understand how good they've got it now."

"More like they're stuck with and afraid of you. The mermaids are damned to be in the Intracoastal with you forever unless someone frees their spirits, which is on my bucket list now that I know there are more sad souls to rescue. I'm sure my sisters would be delighted to help."

"Who are you? Mother Teresa? Why would you want to help them?"

"Because it's the right thing to do. Just like it would be the right thing for you to make sure your niece got the money that you'd hidden, but you've made it clear that you're not focused on helping others."

"You think you know me so well, but you don't. No matter; you'll get to know me very well when you're part of my army." Serena raised her hands, and her long, slender fingers began glowing as if she were going to attack Elaina. But the sea witch had been oblivious to Nancy and Granny Mason's success in capturing the mermaids who had tried to kidnap Clint. The ghostly women stood on guard with Clint and Todd, ready to give her a spoon full of her own medicine.

26

S tanding on the bow of the boat, Nancy whistled in cat-
call fashion. "Howdy, starfish sucker. I hope you're
ready to get sharked. Have you met my friend, Mrs.
Shark? Here, Sharky, Sharky!" The shark swam to the surface
and locked eyes with Serena. Elaina was certain that if the
shark could have spoken, it would have told the mermaid to get
into its belly.

Serena almost stumbled but caught her footing. "No! I'm
not going back inside that creature's slimy stomach! You can't
make me." Holding her glowing hands up again, she fired a
light beam toward Todd, who ducked just in time. Antago-
nizing Serena may not have been wise, but Nancy couldn't help
herself, especially since Serena had tried to hurt Clint. Any
spirit who threatened her family stood little chance of
surviving.

As the sea witch raised her hands again, Elaina sprang into
action, throwing a fishing net on top of her. She knew it
wouldn't do the mermaid any harm, but at least it would
provide a distraction.

"Todd, stay down! Nancy, get her! She's getting ready to

attack again!" Granny Mason materialized next to Elaina and motioned for Nancy to join them. She glided from the bow to the stern, and when she was in place, she whispered, "Get ready, 1-2-3-go!"

The three women began chanting, "Send this spirit away to her cell. Lock her away for good. Do not send her to Heaven or Hell." A gust of wind chilled the air as Granny Mason pointed her hands at the mermaid, sending emerald green bursts of light from her palms to hold Serena in place while the spell began to take effect. Elaina walked in place, hands in pockets, as she watched in horror. What was taking so long? It didn't last time, and they were capturing more than 200 mermaids at once.

Elaina looked over at a frowning Granny Mason. "Why isn't it working? Is there something you need me to do?"

Her grandmother sighed. "I have no idea unless it's because I was on the Other Side for so long. You and Nancy may have to put some more muscle into it."

"Okay, let's repeat the chant again and focus on the shark while we do it. Hopefully, that will work." Staring at the fish, Elaina saw the conch shell mark's glow change from a golden hue to the rich green, matching the light from her grandmother's hands.

"It's starting to work!" Elaina cheered. "Let's repeat it one more time!" Finally, Serena's body glided just over the shark, momentarily suspended midair before swirling into a cloud-like formation and entering the fish's body. "Yasss! She's gone!"

Suddenly, Elaina's heart sank to the bottom of her chest. Where was the fanny pack? Surely they hadn't let Serena take it with her into the depths of the shark's belly. That couldn't be the case. Clint had been holding on to the bag since he retrieved it from the lighthouse. Thankfully, he'd made his way back to the main boat safely, but his hands were empty.

"Um, Clint, please tell me you have the money, and it didn't just vanish into the shark along with that sea demon." *I'm going to puke right now, and I may not stop for a very long time.*

Her brother-in-law showed his empty palms. "I don't have the money. I promise. Cross my heart, hope to die." He crossed his index finger over his heart and smiled.

"Seriously, Clint. The last time I saw it, you had it with you in the dingy. Don't mess around. This isn't the time, and I'm not laughing." He had to be joking. He shook his head and pulled out his empty shorts pockets.

Ugh. This wasn't possible; it was her worst nightmare. Maybe she was asleep. She had to be. These sorts of things didn't happen to normal people. Talking to herself, Elaina paced the wooden deck.

Looking up at her family, Elaina shook her head. "Am I really going to have to bring Serena back out again just to get the money and send her right back? This sucks so bad."

Wearing a sheepish grin, Todd walked up to her and held up the fanny pack by a strap. Elaina's jaw dropped as she grabbed the bag out of his hand. How dare Clint corrupt her sweet, serious Todd! She'd have to pay them back for tricking her. Blake would be only too happy to collaborate on an elaborate practical joke.

Elaina slapped Todd on the shoulder. "No way, babe! Were you going to let me bring back that hag? You almost gave me a heart attack. I'm completely stunned! That's it; Clint is rubbing off on you too much. I'm going to tell Blake that we have to keep you guys separated from now on. Not cool, y'all!"

Clint was doubled over laughing, and his face changed from red to purple. They wouldn't have thought it was funny if she'd released Serena, even for a short time. Besides, didn't they know how exhaustion had taken its toll on this poor, pregnant mama? Elaina didn't have the energy to joke around.

She unzipped the purse to confirm the money was inside. Sure enough, 800 large bills had been crammed into an interior pouch. Serena was probably the first and last person in history to carry around this massive sum of money along with scrunchies, lip gloss and bubble gum inside a fanny pack.

Elaina needed to share the good news. Dialing Glenda's phone number, Elaina's fingers trembled uncontrollably. Everyone had worked so hard to find the money, to make a difference for this kid. But what if they hadn't been fast enough to help Lauren?

When Glenda picked up the phone, Elaina tried to sound cheerful yet soothing. "Hey, how is everything going?" She bit her lip and fidgeted with the zipper on her jacket.

"Very much the same, but she opened her eyes for a bit today. That was a huge win. I just want my baby to get healthy again." Glenda sighed.

"I want the same thing for her. And good news—we found the money! You won't believe what we went through to get it. I'll save the big crazy story for another day. All that matters now is that Lauren is going to get her treatment."

The phone went silent. "Hey, Glenda? Are you still there? Hello?" Elaina bit her lip. Was it a bad connection? Probably. She was on a boat about 20 yards away from Sweetgrass Island, which wasn't exactly civilized—not a cell tower in sight.

"Yes. I'm still here," Glenda whispered. "I just can't believe what you've done for us, and I have no way of understanding why. Heather and I have only done horrible things to you."

"My parents raised us to take care of people, and I could help Lauren in a way that most people couldn't. But more than that, I wanted to. She's a sweet kid, and I'd like nothing more than to see her live a full, healthy life."

Glenda sobbed. "Thank you so much. I don't know what we'd do without you."

Elaina rubbed her tear-filled eyes on her sleeve and sniffed. "It's given me a purpose. We'll get the money to you. Go ahead and make all of her appointments with the specialist!"

Hanging up the phone, she smiled. This was one of the most exciting moments of her life. Lauren stood a chance of seeing her fifteenth birthday now; that meant more than anything else that could be done with $80,000.

More than 30 years ago, Serena had intended to buy a house for her sisters with the money. If she had lived, the money would have been gone. Not that Glenda wanted her sister to die, but since that is how life had played out, Lauren was getting another shot at living. Fate had a funny way of showing its hand at the right time.

27

As Clint drove the boat to the marina, cool, salty air caressed Elaina's skin. She lay her head on Todd's shoulder, letting the tension melt away from her body. The search was over, and the battle had finally ended. Somehow, their family was no worse for the wear. That wasn't typically the case after the Nelson sisters' wars with the supernatural. Elaina knew that grateful didn't quite sum up the vibe.

It seemed unreal that Christmas was a mere two days away. She hadn't even thought about buying anyone gifts, not that they would expect them. Still, she wanted to do something nice for her family, especially her niece and nephew. Blake's daughter, Macy, had grown up so much since last year. At four, she understood presents, Santa Claus, and the magic that came along with both. Brittany's little one was too young to comprehend holiday traditions, but Elaina wanted to spoil him, regardless.

Todd put his arm around her. "I'm so glad that's over. I wasn't sure I'd ever see you again when you went missing. I'd just received the best news in my life—that you were healthy and pregnant with twins." His chest expanded as he drew a deep breath. "The next thing I knew, I was sitting in the car waiting for the nurse to bring you to the portico, but you never came. I waited for 20 minutes before I parked the car and ran into the hospital. I didn't know if something had gone wrong with the babies or if you were sick again. No one could find you, and they said your nurse's shift was over. I had no idea that she was the one who had kidnapped you!"

"None of it matters now, though. It's Christmas, and I want to think of this whole experience as the year we saved a family's holiday season. We're giving them hope. Isn't helping others what the holiday is all about?" Elaina thought about how much her outlook on life had changed. Her focus had shifted from herself and her career to how she could support others.

Todd sighed. "I'm coming to terms with letting these creeps off the hook, but just because it's important to you. And it will help a kid who's been through a hellish life."

"Thank you for understanding where I'm coming from. How should we get this money to Glenda? Lauren is being airlifted to Nashville in the morning, and Glenda is flying with her. It's late, but would you be up for driving home now? We could stop by the hospital, and then, you could make my Christmas wish of sleeping in my own bed come true."

Todd yawned. "That sounds amazing. I've missed having you sleeping next to me. I haven't slept in weeks. I can't imagine how tired you are, babe. Let's go."

"You guys are hilarious and act so old." Clint laughed. "On second thought, get all the sleep you can before your babies are born. You'll never sleep again. I wish I were kidding about that. Okay, you wild and crazy kids, drop me off at the house, and I'll tell the family you'll be back for all the holiday stuff tomorrow. You know if you come in, they're going to talk your ear off, and it will be way too late to leave."

Elaina smiled. "You're probably right. Southern goodbyes take way too long. And, yep, we'll leave our place tomorrow in plenty of time to make sugar cookies with Macy. We made cookies on July 4, and she made me promise I'd help her make them on Christmas, too."

"What can I say? Macy loves her aunts and uncles. She told me you and Brittany are her best friends. And she wants Uncle Todd and Uncle Ryan to teach her how to play disc golf. She saw pictures of you guys playing at the course in Knoxville about six or seven years ago. That kid thinks that everything you do is 'so awesome.' Her words, not mine." Clint flashed them a huge grin.

"Aww! We all love her, too! I can't wait for her to meet the twins. She's going to be such a great big cousin to them." *Sweet little Macy. What a ball of energy!* Just thinking about spending time with her niece exhausted her. Did that mean she wouldn't be able to keep up with her kids? Should she worry? *No.* All the parents she knew said the same thing—you're always exhausted regardless of how much sleep you think you got.

After the couple dropped Clint off at the Mason B&B, they quickly crossed the Isle of Palms Connector and started the two-hour drive up Highway 17 North. Taking a nap would have been wise, but Elaina was trembling too hard to fall asleep. Besides, she needed to help keep Todd alert while he drove.

As they crossed the North Carolina state line, she took a deep breath, mentally preparing herself for going back to the hospital. Seeing Lauren connected to an IV and half a dozen beeping machines the first time had been unnerving. Almost two days had passed since then. What if her face was more drawn and pale, her body more lifeless? *Get your crap together. This isn't about you.*

No one could deny the kid was a fighter. She'd survived more hardships in her 14 agonizing years than many senior citizens had seen in their long, rich lives. Would this girl get to do everything that constitutes a so-called happy life—go to college, start a career, get married, buy a house, have babies and watch her children repeat this beautiful process? Elaina prayed for Lauren. At this point, that's all she could do.

28

Glistening Christmas lights decorated the rooflines throughout downtown Wilmington, and well-lit restaurant windows glowed with the smiles of dressed-up patrons enjoying gatherings with their friends and family. For a moment, Elaina envied them, but she remembered what she was doing tonight had a great purpose. Besides, her time to celebrate the holidays with family would come soon enough.

As Todd parked the Jeep at the hospital, she cleared her mind and breathed in and out slowly. But after everything Elaina had been through, meditating could only help so much. Regardless of Lauren's condition, she had to go to her room and face Glenda and Heather.

"Are you ready to go inside, babe?" Todd kissed her cheek and reached for her hand.

"Yes and no, but I have to be." Elaina sighed. "Give me a second." She unbuckled her seatbelt, opened the door and jumped out of the Jeep. Every movement she made seemed to go in slow motion; things she ordinarily did without noticing stood out like a sore thumb. *Why is adulting so hard?*

Elaina's palms sweat as she walked the winding maze to Lauren's room. She stood frozen at the door until Todd placed his hand on her shoulder. "It's going to be okay. Don't forget we're in this together." His sweet reminder gave her the strength she needed to open the door. There was no changing what was on the other side, anyway.

Nothing could have prepared Elaina for the sight that lay before her—a grinning Lauren reclined in bed, playing cards with a cute young male nurse.

"Oh, my Lord! I can't believe it! When did you wake up?"

Lauren smiled. "Just a few hours ago. A voice kept telling me I needed to pull through for my mom. I don't know if what I heard was real or if I imagined it, but it gave me the strength I needed to find my way back."

Tears sprung from Elaina's puffy eyes. "I'm so relieved. Thank God!" *What a miracle! God truly answers prayers.*

"My mom told me you went through a lot to get money to send me to Nashville for treatments. I don't know what to say other than thank you for caring so much about me. You're going to make a great mom. I mean, if you did something so crazy for someone you just met, imagine what you'll do for your kids. They're already so lucky to have you."

Todd stepped closer to the bed. "I completely agree with you. And I feel pretty lucky to have her, too." *I need to marry this man sooner rather than later.*

Lauren and Todd exchanged introductions, and Elaina hung back in amazement. Even if Glenda had texted her to let her know about Lauren's drastic improvement, Elaina wouldn't have believed her.

"Hey, Lauren, where are your mom and aunt?" Elaina looked around the room, halfway expecting Heather to jump out from a dark corner. That woman gave her an uneasy feeling.

"Aunt Heather went home to get some stuff for us. Mom is in the cafeteria. When she was positive I was doing better, she got out of this room for a few minutes. I can't wait until I can do that." She glared at the nurse, who excused himself and left the room.

"Well, you ran that poor boy off in a hurry!" Todd laughed.

"Oh, he'll be okay. He's just a little dramatic." Lauren rolled her eyes.

Elaina hadn't seen this sassy side of her young friend, but it was refreshing to see the girl acting like a teenager instead of a middle-aged woman in a 14-year-old's body.

"Are you still going to Nashville tomorrow?"

"Yeah, but the doctor said I might not have to be airlifted now. Since Mom is a nurse, he might let Aunt Heather drive us there, which would save a lot of money. And I could put the rest of the cash into a college fund." Lauren's eyes sparkled, giving Elaina the peace she'd been seeking.

There was one more thing Elaina needed to take care of before she left the hospital. She kissed Lauren on the head and told her to send text updates in the morning. The walk to the bank of elevators passed much more quickly this time.

Just before Elaina walked into the cafeteria, Todd pulled her aside and kissed her passionately. Her cheeks flushed as a warm sensation overtook her body. Since her kidnapping, she had forgotten about romance, but now, getting this gorgeous man home was at the top of her mind.

Catching her breath, she smiled. "What was that for?"

"Just because I love you. And, well, I thought it would be a shame to let perfectly good mistletoe go to waste." He pointed to the sprigs of greenery hanging in the hallway near the double doors to the cafeteria.

"Let's hurry and take care of this so that we can get *home*." She gave him a meaningful look. Todd's steady gaze told her he'd picked up on the hint.

He opened the door for her. "After you, babe."

Despite being necessary, refocusing on Glenda had proven to be difficult. Entering the cafeteria, Elaina looked around, trying to find the aging nurse who had changed the course of her life just three weeks prior. It was funny how many people, dead and alive, had affected the Nelson sisters' lives in drastic ways. At least Glenda wasn't as terrifying or unpredictable as Parker, Blake's ex, whose maniacal spirit had tried to harm the entire family more than once. Of course, Heather and Serena gave Parker a run for his money in their own ways.

After walking the perimeter of the cafeteria, Elaina was about to give up on finding Glenda there. Maybe they'd crossed paths without realizing it. The couple had been pretty distracted for several minutes in the hallway. Glenda could have seen them and kept walking, not wanting to disrupt their moment of passion. Although, based on recent experience, that level of consideration didn't seem to be part of her repertoire.

Just when Elaina was about to give up, someone placed their hand on her shoulder. She fought her first instinct to elbow them in the stomach and instead turned around to see Glenda. The previously worn-down-looking mother smiled, her eyes sparkling and her skin radiant. This was probably the first time in years that Glenda had found hope for Lauren's future.

Elaina already felt a connection to her babies and an uncontrollable urge to protect them at all costs. She couldn't imagine the pain Glenda had experienced, but she was proud to help a mother save her child's life. *What an incredible gift!*

Granny Mason, Nancy and Susan had taught the Nelson sisters to help others, regardless of their transgressions. In their family, everyone deserved a second chance. Not all families had these upstanding matriarchs as role models. It was easy to understand how someone who hadn't had such positive influences in life could turn to a dark and evil place. Poor Serena, Glenda and even Heather — they'd grown up without someone who deeply cared about their wellbeing and had taught them right from wrong.

Glenda smiled. "Thank you for coming back tonight. I can't

tell you how much it means to me. We came close to losing my sweet baby earlier today, but something in her changed a few hours ago. It was like someone gave her a pep talk to pull through, and she listened. Whatever happened, I'm so thankful. I can't imagine if ..." Glenda shook her head. "I'm not going to go there. My girl is doing so much better. I can't wait to get her to Nashville so she can start her treatments."

"Speaking of that, here's the money." Elaina gestured to Todd, who handed over the fanny pack.

Holding the purse in her hands, Glenda burst into laughter. "I remember Serena wearing this hideous bag. I thought it was the ugliest purse on the planet, but she insisted on wearing that thing everywhere she went. I wish you could have met her before she died. She was such a caring sister, but it's easy to understand how someone would become bitter after dying in such a tragic way at a young age."

Of course, Elaina agreed that the events surrounding Serena's death were horrific, but did that mean she had to try to kill everyone who crossed her path and try to make them part of their underwater army? *Nope!* But there wasn't a point in arguing with Glenda about it tonight. Besides, Elaina needed to get Todd back home.

After the couple said their goodbyes to Glenda, Todd grabbed Elaina's hand and kissed it. "I can't wait to get home, and there's no pressure from me for anything. I was serious when I said I wanted to sleep with you in our bed. I meant to sleep, nothing else; that is unless you want to, because who am I to argue with a beautiful woman?"

Elaina giggled. "I can't promise what will happen when my head hits the pillow, but let's go see."

Todd raised his eyebrows. "Hmm ... sounds like a plan to me." He opened the passenger side door for Elaina and helped her get inside. Before he closed the door, he leaned in to kiss her again. "I'm so thankful to have you back safe and sound."

Her heart fluttered throughout the drive home. Todd was

trustworthy, loving and made her happy beyond measure. Most importantly, he would make sure their children had everything they needed. She couldn't imagine having a better partner in life and love.

Elaina cried when the Jeep pulled into their driveway. The two-story brick and stucco condo had never been a more welcome sight. Todd jumped out of the Jeep and came around to open her door.

For a moment, he froze in place, staring at her. "You're so beautiful." Those words were incomprehensible. With everything she'd been through, there hadn't been time for worrying about appearances. Love really must be blind; otherwise, he would have already run away.

Todd gave Elaina his hand, leading her to their bedroom. They lay down together, and he wrapped his arms and legs around her. Looking into her eyes, he ran his finger along the outline of her lips. "I've missed this so much. I can't imagine my life without you." He kissed her gently, sending sparks throughout her body.

"Same. You're my person." Elaina kissed him back, allowing her body to melt into his. After a beautiful hour of making love, she thanked God for giving her a loyal, loving man. Romance had never come easily to Elaina until she met Todd in college. They had fallen for each other quickly and stayed together ever since.

Despite all the years together, Todd and Elaina's fire hadn't fizzled out, not even close. Would having children zap their energy and shortchange their time in the bedroom? Probably, but it didn't matter. They'd find a new meaning for love as they built their family.

29

The next morning, Elaina lay in bed, staring at Todd. Sleeping a solid eight hours in their plush bed had refreshed her. It was Christmas Eve and time to go to Isle of Palms to celebrate with the Nelson family. She got up, packed their bags and made toast and coffee before waking him.

"Babe, you didn't have to do all this. I would have packed and made us breakfast, or we could have stopped on our way there. You've been through so much, and you're having our babies. You need to take it easy. Let me take care of you or, at the very least, let me help you."

She waved her hand to dismiss his concern. "I'm fine. I didn't want to bother you. Anyway, you looked so cute cuddled up with the down comforter." When would Todd learn that he couldn't keep her in a bubble throughout her entire pregnancy? Wasn't he the one who'd said the Nelson women were as tough as nails? That assessment was on point.

After eating breakfast, Todd grabbed their bags and turned to Elaina. "Hey, are you almost ready to leave?"

"Yep. I just need to get one more thing." Elaina had almost

forgotten that Blake had asked them to bring dress clothes for family pictures. She ran to her closet and looked through its contents. Toward the back, she found a silver garment bag, which contained a dress she'd bought for a party they hadn't attended. She quickly threw together an outfit for Todd, too, and placed it inside the garment bag.

Locking up their condo, she bit her lip. Something told her change was in the air once again, but she'd learned that it was impossible to avoid progress. If things went according to plan, the changes would be positive and welcome. Having her family nearby made everything easier, but the kidnapping taught her she was strong enough to go it alone when needed.

As they set course for the island, Elaina thought back to the harrowing adventure she had just experienced. She dreaded explaining the details to her parents and sisters. Of course, Clint and Todd had shared some updates with them, but her family would still have a million questions. She didn't want them to worry. They couldn't undo the kidnapping, and Serena had been safely locked away again.

The three-hour drive was relatively uneventful. Elaina asked Todd to take her to Mount Pleasant Towne Centre so that she could buy gifts. "I promise, this will be a quick shopping trip. I'll meet you back at the car in an hour."

After they finished shopping, they got back into the Jeep and crossed the Isle of Palms Connector. She hadn't bought much, just small presents to let everyone know she hadn't forgotten them. When they pulled into the Mason B&B drive-way, Macy burst through the front door and waited for them on the front porch.

Getting out of the car, Elaina called out to her niece. "There's my Macy Bear! Come here, kiddo." The little girl ran and wrapped her arms and legs around Elaina's leg. Ruffling Macy's hair, Elaina told her to go inside and cover her eyes so she wouldn't see her presents. The little girl wrinkled her nose and ran full force into the house.

Elaina laughed as she loaded the shopping bags, the garment bag and her blue quilted overnight tote into her arms. Todd grabbed the rest of their luggage and pointed to the garment bag. "What is that? It looks like an awfully fancy dress bag. Are we going somewhere where we need to dress up that much?"

"Oh, Blake wanted me to bring this party dress with me." Elaina shrugged.

"But I didn't bring a suit or anything nice with me, though." Todd frowned. "I didn't know we were going to dress up."

"Don't worry. Your outfit is in there, too." Elaina smiled, thinking about the blazer, button-down shirt, slacks and tie she'd picked out to go with her dress.

Todd shook his head. "Okay. I could have picked out my own clothes. I just hate that you're doing so much right now. Seriously, take it easy. I know your family is going to agree with me on this one."

Jeremy Nelson poked his head out the front door. "Hey, y'all! What are we going to agree on?"

"That your daughter needs to chill out for the rest of the week and let us help her. Please back me up." Todd gave her a pointed look.

"Yep. I'm with you on that one. And girl, you're never too old to listen to your dad." Jeremy took the stack of bags out of her arms and nudged her into the house. "C'mon. We're gonna get you settled in the living room, and I'll pour you a tall glass of sweet tea with an orange slice, your favorite."

As they entered the house, Blake led Elaina to the sofa. "I'm so glad you're here! Macy has been talking nonstop about making cookies with y'all today."

"She never forgets anything, does she?" Elaina shook her head.

Blake giggled. "Nope. She doesn't. I didn't remind her. And just to warn you, she has a billion questions about the twins— when will they be born; what are you going to name them;

when will they be old enough to play—the list will go on and on."

Elaina pursed her lips. "I wouldn't expect any less. We're going to have a great time hanging out together."

Jeremy pointed his finger at her. "You can hang out with whoever you want as long as you're sitting or lying down. You can't be chasing a four-year-old around the whole dang house. Todd asked us to help you relax, and we're gonna do it. Ya hear me?"

She saluted. "Got it, Dad. I promise not to have a wild and crazy rave with Macy. We're just making Christmas cookies. No biggie."

"You let me know when you're ready, and I'll set you up at the kitchen table."

Goodness–they really wouldn't let her be. It probably was a good idea to let her body recuperate after all the trauma it had undergone recently. One upside was that she wouldn't have to clean up the mess after cutting out and decorating cookies.

"I guess now is just as good of a time as any. Blake, you wanna grab Macy?" Elaina walked to the kitchen, and Jeremy followed behind with a small ottoman and a throw pillow. When she sat down at the table, he placed the pillow to support her back and the ottoman under her feet. She thanked him, and he kissed the top of her head before retreating to the living room.

Macy came barreling down the steps, singing the ABCs at the top of her lungs, adding vibrato to the end of the tune. That kid sure was rambunctious, to put it mildly, but the entire family loved her to pieces. She had the purest heart and an unusually sweet disposition compared to most kids her age.

"Auntie 'Laina, Mama took me to get new cookie cutters. I want to make snowmen and stars. What do you want to make?"

Elaina looked through Blake's baking tin, which had been filled with decorating equipment. She pulled out some cookie cutter options. "What about Santa Claus and his reindeer? That way, you can leave some yummy cookies for Santa when he comes to bring your presents. What do you think?"

Macy sat still with her index finger and thumb on her chin, definitely a gesture she'd picked up from Clint's body language. It was rare to see her niece speechless, but Elaina knew it wouldn't last for long. She could see the wheels turning in the child's head.

"Yep, yep. That is good. If Santa likes the cookies, he will leave me lots of presents."

"What presents do you want the most, kiddo?"

Macy looked over her shoulder and motioned for Elaina to come closer. This move had Clint written all over it, too. "I told Santa Claus at the mall. Don't tell Mommy or Daddy, but I want a baby sister or brother."

Elaina laughed. "Um, your Mommy and Daddy are the ones who decide if that's something they want, so maybe you should tell them instead of me."

"But I can't tell them because the magic needs to happen in Mommy's belly." Macy waved her fingers and danced in her booster chair.

Puzzled, Elaina decided not to push the issue. "What else do you want from Santa Claus?"

"Snow! Lots of pretty, sparkly snow to make real snowmen and snow angels in, and I want to eat snowflakes on my tongue."

Elaina smiled weakly. Macy wanted two things that no one had much control over. Clint and Blake wanted to have a second child, but Elaina hadn't talked to them about it since Blake had confessed their plans to conceive. For all she knew, they'd experienced fertility issues. Having a baby was a personal matter that Elaina was afraid to broach with her sister.

To make matters worse for Macy's wish list, Charleston hadn't seen a white Christmas since the Nelson sisters were little. Damn, this kid had a tall order. What could she do to give this kid one of the things she'd requested? Surely, she wanted something else.

"Hey, kiddo. Don't you want a new doll, a bike, some connective building blocks or a board game? Something Santa could pick up from the store?"

"Nope. Just the baby and the snow. Doh-de-doh." Macy snapped her fingers in time to her little tune. *Oh, geez. Maybe Granny or Nancy can help make some snow, even just a little sprinkle in front of one window for a couple of minutes.*

Elaina scooted away from the table and walked to the bathroom. Closing the door behind her, she called out for the matriarchal spirits. "Hey, guys, I need you right now." She waited a few minutes, and when they didn't show up, she tried again. Tapping her fingers on the vanity, "Y'all, I need your help with Macy. Please come." Washing her face, she looked up in the mirror to see a silvery mist appear behind her. She breathed a sigh of relief after Nancy and Granny Mason materialized out of thin air.

Nancy spun around in a circle and curtsied. "You rang, hon?"

Granny Mason shushed her. "Nan, this might be serious. It's about Macy." She turned to Elaina. "Is she okay? What's going on?"

"She's fine, but this is the first year she has really understood who Santa Claus is and the concept of gift-giving. The only things she has asked for are snow and a baby brother or sister. You know as well as I do that I can't do anything about either of those wishes, but I thought y'all might be able to work some magic on the snow part. Or maybe you could talk to the man upstairs for help?"

"But what do Blake and Clint think about having another baby? Shouldn't that be their choice?" Granny Mason asked wide-eyed.

Elaina laughed. "Of course. I wasn't suggesting that you have anything to do with that mess. On the other hand, if you can help, Blake told me they've been trying to conceive. They'd be stoked."

Nancy's blue eyes sparkled. "They wouldn't be the only ones who would be excited. I've dreamed about this day for so long. Oh, Julia Caroline, you have to admit that Macy would make a great big sister. She's so loving and attentive with Willow."

"I definitely agree it would be sweet, but tending to a dog is much different from having a baby around. I'd feel better if I at least talked to Blake before I mess with her affairs. I'll try to pull her aside tonight."

Looking at her watch, she realized it was time to cook dinner. She walked to the kitchen, where her mom and sisters were peeling potatoes and opening canning jars of green beans. She stirred the crockpot of chicken and dumplings that Blake had made earlier that day and slid a cookie sheet covered in biscuits into the oven. When everything was ready, the Nelson women filled bowls with the food and placed them on the kitchen table.

At dinner, a stillness overtook the kitchen as the entire family ate in an odd silence. Even Macy shoveled mashed potatoes into her mouth without saying a word. What in the heck was going on with her typically boisterous family? Elaina scanned the room for signs of illness or extreme exhaustion. Everyone's skin had a normal, healthy glow. There weren't any bags under anyone's eyes.

"What gives you guys? Why is everyone so quiet? It makes me think you're up to something." Elaina narrowed her eyes.

Her mom laughed. "We're just enjoying a nice, quiet Christmas Eve dinner. What's so weird about that?" She paused. "Oh, never mind. I can't even pretend that's normal for us, but it's none of your business. You should help Macy write her letter to Santa and get to bed. Tomorrow's gonna be a long day."

Elaina's eyes widened. "Okay, Mom. Way to make dinner

even more strange." The whole family was in on some big secret. When it came to gifts, Elaina preferred surprises, whether she was the one giving or receiving the present. So, if that's the way her family wanted to play it, she'd follow along.

After helping Macy write her wish list, they set out cookies and milk for Santa and a plate of baby carrots for the reindeer. Macy grabbed Elaina's hand and led her upstairs. "Time for bed. We can't be awake, or Santa won't come!"

"You're absolutely right. I'm so glad you listened when your mom and dad told you that." Elaina tucked her niece into bed and kissed her forehead. "I love you, kiddo. Nighty night."

"Love you, Auntie 'Laina! Now it's sleepy time, so that Santa will come!" Macy blew a kiss and forced her eyes closed. *What a cute kid!* Next Christmas, she and Todd would have their own little ones. They'd be too little to understand the gift-giving and Santa portion of the holiday, but the time for that would come soon enough. And the gifts weren't the important part, anyway.

Elaina walked to her bedroom and collapsed onto the bed. Whatever Christmas wishes came true tomorrow, one thing was for sure—the Nelson sisters' lives were constantly changing.

30

At 5:30 in the morning, Elaina woke to the sound of little feet thundering across the hardwood floors in the hallway, followed by a tiny voice proclaiming, "It's Christmas, everybody! Time to wake up!" *Ugh! Why did I complain about the quiet last night?*

Todd sat up in bed and yawned. "I guess we're getting a preview of what we have to look forward to with our kids. What do you think, should we get up? On the one hand, the four-year-old is telling a house full of adults what to do, but on the other, it's Christmas, and we love Macy."

Elaina scrunched her face and groaned. "It's so early, but I guess you're right. We should go have the whole experience. She's such a great kid, and we should spoil her as much as possible."

"Exactly. Isn't that our job as Macy's aunt and uncle?"

Todd had a point. Elaina pulled on a fluffy red robe over her buffalo plaid pajamas and stepped into her favorite pair of shearling-lined slippers. *Let's see whose wishes came true today.*

They walked downstairs to the living room to see most of the family sitting on the floor around the Christmas tree. Elaina took a seat on the couch just behind Blake and watched Macy run from one gift to the next to check the name tag for her name. Clint and Blake had done a great job teaching her to read at an early age. Macy would be several steps ahead of other kids in her grade when she started school.

As her niece opened presents, Elaina couldn't help but watch in awe. The child had asked for miracles, not gifts, yet she expressed deep gratitude for every package she opened. She even exclaimed that she'd "always wanted" the yellow rain jacket and boots Brittany gave her. It was an adorable sight for sure.

Macy hadn't questioned why Santa didn't bring her the gifts she'd asked for in her letter. Spoiled wasn't the right word to describe the kid. Elaina couldn't love her niece any more than she already did, but that didn't mean the little girl didn't impress her with her maturity and kindness every day.

Elaina gazed out the window and noticed something about the scenery that looked different. When a squirrel ran past the motion-enabled security light, the difference was more apparent. Everything had been covered in a blanket of white. Her memories of the last Lowcountry Christmas snow were fuzzy, but a warm sensation filled her body every time she tried to reminisce about that day.

Having been only three years old, what she remembered most was her dad laughing as he pulled them around in a sled and the hot chocolate their mom had made them after they came back inside the house. Her hot chocolate was the best; she always added a handful of miniature marshmallows, topped with colorful decorating sugars and her *secret* ingredient—a kiss. Now it was Macy's turn to make these memories; she had gotten her wish!

"Hey, Macy! Go get your coat and some warm clothes on, quick!" Her niece looked at the toys in her hands, but nodded and ran to her room.

A few minutes later, she returned to the living room,

wearing a puffy purple coat, a clashing red and green plaid scarf, leopard print leggings, and her new yellow rain boots. Elaina stifled a giggle. The outfit choice would make for some interesting snow day pictures—no need to rain on Macy's parade. Instead, Elaina grabbed her niece's hand and took her outside. The rest of the family followed behind, cameras in hand.

Macy's eyes widened as she walked into the winter wonderland. She'd only seen snow on TV. Blake and Clint had planned to take her to the mountains to see it first hand at some point this winter, but it had come to the island, no doubt thanks to Granny Mason and Nancy. Elaina didn't know how they'd pulled off this massive blanket of snow, but it didn't matter. She'd rather keep the mystery alive. It was in moments like these that adults could appreciate the magic of Christmas as much as children.

Clint came running from the gardening shed, smiling ear to ear, with a hot pink sled in hand. "I'd bought this for our trip to the mountains. I had no idea we'd get to use it at home on Christmas!"

"He may be even more enthusiastic about the snow than Macy!" Blake laughed. But the sparkle in her sister's eyes told Elaina she was excited, too.

"I can't wait to do this with the twins someday!" Todd put his arm around Elaina, and her heart fluttered at the thought as she watched Clint pull Macy around in the fluffy white snow, and the child's laughter filled the backyard. What a memorable day for her niece to look back on as an adult.

Macy would be seven or eight years old by the time the twins were old enough to sled. If Clint and Blake didn't have another baby soon, their children would have a huge age gap. Would they get to play together, or would Macy think she was too much older and cooler than this imaginary baby? What if the baby was real? No one had asked Blake if Macy's other Christmas wish had come true.

Elaina stared at her sister. "Did you talk to Granny Mason last night?"

Blake nodded and smiled. "Yep, but I didn't need her help. I was waiting to tell everyone during dinner today. I went to the doctor a few days ago. I'm eight weeks along."

"I'm so freaking excited! I can't wait until Macy knows." This news was the best Christmas gift their family had ever received.

"Oh, Macy was the one who told me I was having a baby. It was so weird how matter of fact she was when she told me. I didn't believe her at first, but I took a pregnancy test, and sure enough, she was right."

"So, her Christmas wish was for something she already knew was happening?" *That kid!* Elaina had to laugh.

"Yep, but she wants this baby." Blake placed her hands on her belly.

"Do you think she has a gift for knowing things like this?"

"Maybe. At least this ability won't put Macy in danger. I dread the day when she has to fight her first evil spirit. I hope I can be there to protect her." Macy had her first encounter with malevolent ghosts last year, but thankfully, they had saved the battle for Brittany, Blake and Elaina.

"We'll all be there if and when it happens," Elaina reassured her sister. After all, Macy was a Nelson girl through and through. Her last name might be Parsons, but the Nelson sisters and their children would always stick together through thick and thin.

31

After a day filled with playing in the snow, the family gathered in the dining room for an early dinner. The mango-hued sun filtered throughout the room, bathing every surface in a warm glow. Elaina loved these glorious island sunsets, and the one today was exceptionally brilliant as it reflected off the sparkling white ground.

Blake rose from the table. "Hey, we have one more surprise that I think everyone is going to enjoy, but there's one part you won't like about it. You're going to need to get dressed up so we can take pictures." Everyone groaned in unison. "Trust me. It will be worth it. And Elaina, now would be the time for you to wear that party dress that you brought."

Elaina stared at her sister, knowing she was up to something, although she wasn't sure what. If she weren't already engaged, she'd swear that Todd had planned some elaborate proposal. However, they'd been engaged for months, and he wasn't one to make a big show of things. Loving surprises, Elaina played along.

She ran upstairs and slipped on the midi-length silver party dress with matching silver flats. Her wavy auburn hair was a bit of a mess, so she twisted it into an updo and placed a crystal-encrusted headband in front of the mound of fluffy curls on her head. *Not half bad for a horrible hair day!* The finishing touch was Granny Mason's pearl and diamond chandelier earrings.

Todd opened the door and gasped. "You look so beautiful, babe!" He ran over to kiss her, lingering longer than she'd expected. "Do we have time to ... you know?"

"No, silly! I love you, but we've got to get downstairs. I'm betting Blake wants to get the sunset in the pictures, so there's no time for anything. Hurry and change." She felt bad for dismissing him so quickly. "Hey, I promise we'll make time for each other tonight."

"Deal." He arched an eyebrow, giving her a meaningful look.

Elaina shook her head and checked on Macy to make sure she'd changed out of her muddy play clothes. Walking into her niece's bedroom, she wasn't expecting to see Macy lying on the floor, covered in a bright blue marker.

"What on earth have you done?" Elaina threw her hands up in the air. "Your mom is going to be so disappointed."

"Why do you say that?"

Elaina turned around to see Blake, wearing a sparkly red cocktail dress, standing in the doorway. "Apparently, I need to move out of the way so you can check out your daughter's handiwork." As she inched away from Macy, Blake's jaw dropped.

"Macy Caroline Parsons, what in blue blazes would possess you to do that?"

The girl titled her head. "I saw Auntie Elaina putting on makeup, and I wanted to look as pretty as her."

"Oh, geez. Don't get me into trouble, kiddo." Elaina laughed. "C'mon, we'll scrub you down really quick." Elaina took Macy to her bathroom and told her to get in the shower. "Use your mom's loofah to clean your skin."

The off-key falsetto singing coming from the other side of

the shower curtain told Elaina her niece was okay. After a few minutes, Elaina cleared her throat.

"Macy Bear, is your skin nice and clean yet?"

A tiny hand poked out of the shower and waved. "Yep, yep! All clean!" Elaina rolled her eyes. She loved this kid, but she sure was a handful sometimes.

"Okay, let's go, kiddo. Time to put on your Christmas dress!" She helped Macy get out of the shower and wrapped her in a child-sized terry-cloth robe before leading her niece to her bedroom. "Your mom put your dress on the bed. Put on your panties, slip on your dress, and I'll help you zip up the back." For once, the child got dressed in record time and sat still while Elaina helped her slip on her tights and shoes.

Blake came into the room to check on them. "Wow, you're getting some great practice for being a mom today. Thanks to Macy." She ruffled the girl's hair and smiled.

"Yep, I used the marker and sang the song in the shower just like you told me, Mommy. Can I have a cookie now?" Macy grinned and raised her eyebrows.

Elaina put her hands on her hips. "What do you mean, Macy? Mommy told you to do those things?" Her niece nodded and giggled. "What gives, Blake?"

Blake wouldn't make eye contact with her. "Don't ask me any more questions. Just meet me in the living room in five minutes." While glaring at her sister's back as she slipped through the bedroom door with Macy, Elaina wondered why Blake, the photography perfectionist, would want to waste a magnificent sunset for her photoshoot. There wasn't an obvious reason, so Blake must have a fascinating secret. But what could it be? She'd already shared the news of her pregnancy with the family. Elaina pulled out her cell phone and set a timer, so she wouldn't keep checking the time.

32

Elaina paced the hardwood floors in Macy's bedroom. The suspense was eating away at her; this Christmas surprise must be pretty huge. Otherwise, why would Blake go through all this effort? When the timer on her cell phone rang, she ran downstairs and looked for her sister in the kitchen and living room.

"Blake? Where the heck are you? I'm ready. You can't keep this from me anymore."

Her dad walked out of the downstairs powder room. "Hey, gorgeous. Your sister sent me to get you, but I had to straighten my bowtie. Does it look okay?" Her dad's goofy smile didn't match his serious outfit—a blazer, bowtie, button-down shirt, pressed khakis and wingtip shoes.

Elaina resisted the urge to laugh at the juxtaposition and linked arms with him. "You look handsome." She kissed his cheek, and her dad dabbed at his eyes with a handkerchief. "Dad, what's wrong? Are you okay?"

He cleared his throat. "You girls are just so grown up. I remember when you were Macy's age. Now, you're starting your own families, and not only that, y'all have some incredible careers. I'm proud of all of you." Elaina's heart sank when he wiped his eyes again and apologized. "I didn't mean to get emotional."

She hugged him and rubbed his shoulder. "It's okay. I don't know what's bringing this on, but I love you, Dad! Now, if you're okay, let's go see what Blake is cooking up outside."

After Elaina stepped onto the screened-in porch, she was put under the spell of the hundreds of white lights that decorated the live oaks and trailed down the strands of Spanish moss. Clint, Todd and Ryan stood in front of one side of a tree, and her sisters and Macy stood on the other. Elaina's mom, Todd's parents and other family members filled about 20 chairs, divided in half by a narrow aisle. *Oh, my God! My family planned the quiet Christmas wedding I'd dreamed about before being kidnapped!*

Clint could perform wedding ceremonies as a justice of the peace, which had come in handy more than once for their family. He raised his eyebrows at Elaina, and she nodded to let him know she was good with what was happening. What would her family have done if she'd run away instead of proceeding down the aisle holding onto her father's arm?

With her pulse racing, she struggled to force a smile, but then, Todd's beaming face put her at ease. This was the man she was about to marry, and soon, they'd have twins! Three months ago, she wouldn't have guessed that this would be the way her wedding would unfold. But the garden was more beautiful than ever, and the people she loved the most were there. That was all that mattered.

A gentle breeze swept across the garden, bringing with it a shimmering, silvery mist and a smiling Granny Mason and Nancy. Elaina blew them a kiss and wiped away a happy tear before proceeding down the aisle toward Todd.

When her grandmother's earrings brushed against her cheek, Elaina flashed back for a quick glimpse into Julia Caroline's memories. She paused on one of Papa reading the story of the Nativity from the Bible. In this memory, Elaina and her sisters, aged 5, 7 and 10, had clung to their grandfather's every word.

But seeing the moment from Julia Caroline's perspective gave Elaina a whole new take on the word, "adoration." Her grandparents' unconditional love for each other had set the tone for generations of great romances. Jeremy and Susan Nelson had undoubtedly followed suit, as had each of their daughters.

Elaina blinked, returning to the present to see the faint silhouette of a man standing beside Granny Mason, with his arm around her. Papa had come back to Palm Court, if only for tonight. Yet again, her grandparents had showed up to support Elaina.

In the Nelson family, December 25 was a day to give thanks for God's gifts — including the greatest gift of all, his Son. Bursting with happiness, Elaina realized she couldn't count her blessings on one hand.

This year, she was grateful for her growing family, the opportunity to help someone in need and the holiday magic that had brought a white Christmas to Palm Court.

ABOUT THE AUTHOR

Stephanie Edwards has been writing professionally since she landed her first newspaper column at the age of 13. Her love for the Lowcountry, the Atlantic Ocean and a good ghost story inspired her to write her first book, The Haunting on Palm Court: An Isle of Palms Suspense.

A stay at a beach cottage with a spooky backyard, filled with old oak trees helped Stephanie bring her book to life. She released the second book in the Isle of Palms Suspense series in May 2021 and is excited to share Christmas on Palm Court with readers, just in time for the holidays!

Stephanie lives in Tennessee with her husband, Ron, and their adorable dog, Shadow. Be sure to keep up with publication dates, events, and other news at www.stephedwardswrites.com.

ALSO BY STEPHANIE EDWARDS

The Haunting on Palm Court

Return to Palm Court

Pearls of Wisdom: An adult coloring book

9 781735 169163